Sunset Cove

Sunset Cove

M. Jean Pike

Steve,
I hope you
enjoy spending the
holidays with your "friends"
at Shadow Lake.
Merry
Christmas!
Jean
12/2011

Black Lyon Publishing, LLC

SUNSET COVE
Copyright © 2011 by M. JEAN PIKE

Our books may be ordered through your local bookstore or by visiting the publisher:

www.BlackLyonPublishing.com

Black Lyon Publishing, LLC
PO Box 567
Baker City, OR 97814

This is a work of fiction. All of the characters, names, events, organizations and conversations in this novel are either the products of the author's vivid imagination or are used in a fictitious way for the purposes of this story.

ISBN-10:   1-934912-41-7
ISBN-13:   978-1-934912-41-6
Library of Congress Control Number: 2011940046

Written, published and printed in
the United States of America.

Black Lyon Contemporary Romance

For my sister, Belinda, who turned the darkness into light.
Your courage inspires me.

Acknowledgements:

I would like to express my heartfelt thanks to my amazing niece, Adina McCoy, who helped me to unlock the mind of a teenaged girl. The song lyrics contained within this story (U Lied, I'm at War) are hers.

My thanks also goes out to Vonda Lee Morton at Lauren's Wildlife Rescue www.Laurenswildliferescue.org for answering my many questions and for helping me to think outside the box of my own experience. That being said, any errors regarding the care and rehabilitation of songbirds found within these pages are mine alone.

And finally, thanks to my dear friend, "Miss Joyce," who cheered me on every step of the way in the writing of this book. I'm not sure I could have done it without you.

Chapter One

On the afternoon of her fifteenth birthday, Maxine Holley devised a five-year plan for her life. She was sitting in Home Economics at the time, listening to Mrs. Warner instruct the class on the proper way to select draperies, when it occurred to her that she wanted to be the sort of woman who had draperies in her windows, rather than faded bed sheets. And that if she wanted to have a happy life, it was up to her to make it happen.

The simple truth of it hit her like a lightning bolt, and she pulled a sheet of paper from the back of her three-ring notebook and went to work on her master plan.

Phase One: Make it through the last three years of high school intact.

She thought of Sheila Cunningham, whisked away from the halls of Hope Haven High School, leaving a whirlwind of whispers in her wake. And of Tracy Rodgers, who married hastily at age sixteen, giving birth just six months later to a "premature" nine-pound baby. Sheila and Tracy would grow up to be bed sheet sort of women, for certain.

Of course, Maxine wanted children. What normal, American girl didn't? But for the first five years, motherhood didn't fit into her plan. She wouldn't end up saddled with some Townie, a baby in each arm. She wouldn't settle for a life of Friday night dances at the fire hall followed by Saturday morning swap meets in the church basement. She wouldn't end up like her mother. Maxine was going to leave the Shadow Lake community forever. Or at least, move to the right section of it.

The lights went dim. Glancing up, she saw that Mrs. Warner

had put a lesson on the overhead projector, some sort of worksheet on identifying proper fabrics. It was nothing that required her immediate attention, so she continued her furtive scribbling.

Phase Two: Get a good job as a bank teller. She thought for a moment, and then added, or a salesgirl at Newberry's Department Store.

She chewed the end of her pencil, deep in thought.

Phase Three: Night School. Earn a typing certificate. Or learn to become a court stenographer.

Phase Four: Get a fabulous job in New York City. Rent a penthouse apartment with a view of the skyline. Meet a rich, handsome fellow (a business man or a lawyer, depending on certificate.)

She smiled, caught up in her lovely daydream. She'd fall in love and have the perfect wedding, with red roses on the altar and a toile gown like the one she'd seen in the J. C. Penney catalogue. She'd be the kind of woman with draperies in every window and wall-to-wall carpeting on the floors. Satisfied with her plan, she tucked the page in the back of her notebook and turned her attention to Mrs. Warner's lesson.

Five years came and went. At twenty, Maxine was still living in her parent's house on Crooked Gate Drive. She was still intact, still sweating out forty long hours a week at the fish canning factory, where she'd taken a job as a quality control inspector in hopes of earning money for college.

Another five years slipped away, and she fell madly in love with Willie Perkins, the day shift foreman at the factory, a Townie she'd known since the second grade. They married in a small ceremony at St. Paul's Lutheran Church. Maxine wore her mother's gown and carried a spray of white baby's breath and miniature pink carnations.

After their honeymoon, she and Willie pooled their savings and bought a small, weather-beaten house on Wisteria Lane, and Maxine knew she would never leave the dank, fish smelling squalor of Sunset Cove. So she hung draperies in the windows of her tumbledown house and chose to be happy.

At thirty-five, she and Willy accepted the cold, hard truth that they would never have a child of their own. So Maxine spread a fresh coat of eggshell paint on the walls of her lavender nursery and applied to the county to take in foster children. Fifteen more years sped past, and Maxine and Willy raised seven boys. Big, loud boys and small, timid boys. All of her boys were lovely, and loveliest of all was Chase.

As she crept down the hallway, her thoughts wandered back to the night Chase had come to them as a four-year-old; an undersized boy with the most incredible blue eyes she'd ever seen. He was their first foster child, and the king of their hearts. A kind, energetic boy, Chase was remarkably sweet-tempered, considering what he'd been through in his young life. His case file had broken Maxine's heart to pieces and she'd known she'd spend the rest of her days trying to make up for all the pain and injustice life had dealt him. The trauma seemed to have left him unable to cry, and the social worker had cautioned Maxine that Chase's hidden wounds were bound to manifest in outward displays sooner or later, and Max kept an ever vigilant eye out for warning signs of trouble that never came. Chase was the love of her and Willy's lives. He'd taught them what it meant to be parents, and from little league to his learner's permit, Maxine had loved every moment of being his mother.

As a child, he spent countless hours playing cops and robbers. He'd taken Criminal Justice classes in high school, and then left them at age eighteen to go off to the police academy. For the first five years there had been frequent phone calls, newsy letters about life in the big city, life as a police officer. In the next five years, their contact dwindled to phone calls on her and Willy's birthdays, Christmas cards with fifty-dollar bills tucked inside. He'd shown up for Willy's funeral two years ago, a strapping, handsome man that she barely recognized. After the memorial service they'd embraced and parted ways again, promising to stay in touch. She hadn't heard from him since. Until he called her four days ago, on Thanksgiving Day.

She hesitated outside his bedroom door and couldn't resist cracking it open to peek inside. He was sprawled out on a bed that seemed much too small for him, one heavily muscled arm thrown over his face. His hair was messy and overgrown. A slight frown worried the corners of Maxine's lips. He'd always been particular about his hair.

At the corner of his eye, a scar was still faintly visible, one he'd received as an eight-year-old when he'd fallen off his bicycle. Her heart overflowed with pride and she smiled. Her lovely little boy had become a beautiful man.

Making her way to the kitchen, she started a pot of coffee. Later she would prepare his favorite feast; bacon, eggs, and chocolate chip pancakes. But not yet. It was barely six a.m. No decent hour to be clattering around.

Still, she made a quick check of the cupboards, just to be certain she had everything she needed. Oh, but it would be nice to have someone to cook for again. Willy's passing had left a cavernous hole in her life. Willy, her Willy, whisked away in his prime, taken without warning. Her eyes clouded with tears, and she swiped at them with a dishcloth. *Stop living in the past, Max,* she thought. *The past is over and done. All you have is today. Make the most of it.*

She poured a cup of coffee and carried it to the table. Outside her window, a pair of chickadees scampered across the snow-covered earth in search of sustenance. The birds reminded her of that night's Sialia Society meeting. It was Glenda's turn to provide refreshments, but Maxine had heard the poor soul had fallen and broken her ankle. She made a mental note to call Polly Church later and offer to bring a coffee cake.

Sipping her coffee, she thought how strange and wonderful life was.

Chase, showing up on her doorstep three days ago. She thought of his shaggy hair, the beard stubble that peppered his face, and a small shadow of worry crossed her heart. He hadn't given her a reason for his visit, had said only that he needed a place to stay for a little while. She stirred her coffee, deep in thought. He'd fallen flat, she supposed. Fallen flat and all she could do was pick him up and dust him off the best she could, like when he'd tumbled from his bicycle all those years ago. As to the specifics, she could only wonder. But sooner or later he'd tell her. The truth of it would come out. All in good time.

Chapter Two

At six-fifteen AM, shivering in her secondhand coat, Lacy Kennedy stepped out the front door of her apartment house. She paused to admire the pristine coat of snow that blanketed the street. Incredible, she thought. Damned near beautiful. Or at least, as close to beautiful as her neighborhood came.

To an outsider, Wisteria Lane might sound like a lovely place to live. Its name conjured up a pretty pathway lined with small, neat cottages, masses of purple blossoms tumbling gently across arbors and picket fences. In reality, Wisteria Lane was a narrow, rutted street in Sunset Cove, its homes a haphazard collection of tired out dwellings with blistering paint. The few houses that were painted, were painted bright, gaudy colors. The kinds of colors poor people used to infuse a bit of cheer into their lackluster lives. Up and down the lane, every other street lamp was broken, and those that worked only served to shed pools of dim, yellow light on the crazily tilting sidewalks.

Arbor Street, the main thoroughfare, consisted of a handful of Mom 'n Pop businesses that hung on by the threads of luck and sheer determination. It wasn't an area the summer tourists visited, or were even aware of. Sunset Cove was hidden away, Lacy thought, like a poor cousin the lake community was ashamed of, but stuck with nonetheless. The rich people lived in areas like Sackett's Harbor and Cardinal Bay. Sunset Cove was where the Townies lived.

In summer, a dank, fishy smell permeated the neighborhood, and the Townies went about their business, pretending not to notice. In winter cruel, white winds howled across the lake, and they shivered with cold and poverty. But in the early morning hours, when all was still and quiet and the first snowfall of the season lay sparkling on the ground, the neighborhood almost redeemed itself. This is what Lacy was thinking as she turned and hurried down the street.

After three blocks her eyes watered and each breath she took was frigid torture. Crossing Cottage Street, she stepped out of the cold and into the tepid warmth of Louie's News Stand. As the buzzer above the door announced her arrival, Louie looked up from the stack of newspapers he was sorting. He grinned. "Morning, young lady."

"Morning, Louie." She shook the snow from her long, brown hair and blew on her hands to warm them before moving to the cappuccino machine. Grabbing a Styrofoam cup from the stack, she placed it beneath the slot labeled 'Caramel Cream' and pushed the button. Lacy's mouth watered in anticipation as the machine began its whooshing and gurgling. Her morning cup of cappuccino was one of the few extravagances she allowed herself in life.

"Off to work today?" Louie asked, not so much a question as a way of making conversation. After four years, he knew her routine as well as she did.

"Yep." She snapped a lid onto her cup and carried it to the front counter.

"And will you be needing a lottery ticket?"

"You know it, brother."

He pulled a play card from the stack behind the counter and handed it to her, watching as she penciled in her lucky numbers. "The jackpot is up to two-point-five million," he said, grinning. "Wouldn't that be a nice chunk of change?"

"Wouldn't it, though." She handed him the ticket, thinking wistfully of the life she could have, if only.

He ran the numbers through the machine and handed her back a ticket. "Don't forget your friends, when these numbers of yours finally pay off."

A deep, throaty laugh bubbled up from inside of her. "How could I forget you, Louie? You're my coffee man!"

He grinned again, a hint of a blush tinting his weathered face. "Off you go, then. Stay warm out there."

She paid for her coffee and ticket, pocketed her change, and walked out, bracing herself against the cold. The weekly Lottery ticket was another extravagance, though unlike the cappuccino,

Lacy thought of it as a necessity. It was the ticket to a life she desperately wanted. If only ...

Not if, Lacy, she reminded herself sharply. *When.*

Three years before, Lacy had attended a lecture at the local library on Attracting Money with Mind Power. The woman presenting the lecture had been as dynamic as she was beautiful. She'd made Lacy believe that if she only concentrated hard enough on something, made herself actually see it, her subconscious mind would make it happen. Every week since, she'd picture herself listening to the radio as the winning Lottery numbers were announced. Two. Seven. Four. Twenty-nine. Fifty-four. Fifty-eight. Her lucky numbers. Her ticket to a better life. She sighed. Three long years. She thought she would have been there by now.

She turned down Arbor Street, cradling the cup in her hands, taking small sips, making it last. In the second block, between a pawn shop and the Penny Pincher Thrift Store, stood the object of her desire. Stopping again, she peered in the window of the empty bakery. The forgotten debris of failed businesses lay scattered in the shadows beside the long counter. Closing her eyes, Lacy imagined the walls painted golden yellow; saw the pastries arranged in glass cases on the counter, a row of customers queued up in front of them. She imagined herself smiling as she rang up their purchases. Above the door hung a sign: A Taste of Heaven: Out of this world pastries!

Her gaze wandered longingly to the For Sale sign in the corner of the window. It had appeared there one morning, nearly a year ago. The agent's name and phone number had long since faded, but Lacy knew them by heart. Mary Nevinger. Two. Seven. Four. One. Eight. Two. Nine. Five out of seven were her lucky numbers. Surely that was a sign from the Universe.

Oh, how she longed to make that call.

Across the lake, a factory whistle mourned the coming hour. With her daydream shattered, she turned and trudged the last three blocks to the Coffee Cup Diner, where she'd waited tables for the past four years.

Four years of spinning my wheels, she mused. *But I'm getting there.*

Lacy was just nineteen years old when Angel went to jail and she'd had to recreate her life. She'd started waiting tables part time at the Coffee Cup while earning her GED at night. Within a year she was full-time at the diner and earning enough money that she'd been able to move out of the homeless shelter and into a low-rent apartment on Wisteria Lane. In the three years since, she'd worked her way up to head waitress, and had persuaded Doreen, the owner, to let her do some of the baking. The lemon meringue pies and apple turnovers she created each morning were as close as she'd come to fulfilling her dream. But I'm getting there, she reminded herself, as she slid her key into the lock and pushed open the front door.

Shrugging out of her coat, she walked through the stillness of the dining room to the kitchen out back, where a soft pool of light flooded beneath the partially closed office door. Creeping toward it, she peeked inside and was surprised to see Doreen sitting behind her desk. The empty coffee cup in front of her told Lacy her boss had been there for awhile.

"What are you doing here?" she asked.

Doreen regarded her from over the top of her tortoise shell reading glasses. "Last I knew I owned the place."

"But Monday's your day off."

"It was, before all hell broke loose. Now I'm filling in for Tommy as cook."

"I thought I was filling in for Tommy today."

"That was sooo yesterday." Doreen gave her a tired smile. "I need you to help cover the dining room, hon. Brittany quit last night."

"She quit? How come?"

Doreen pinched the bridge of her nose between her fingers, a sure sign that one of her migraines loomed on the horizon. "She sent me a text at ten p.m., said she was on her way to South Carolina and wouldn't be coming in. Today or ever. Can you believe that crap?"

"Another one bites the dust."

"It bites, all right. I invested hours in training that girl." She sighed. "Anyway, I've got everything prepped for breakfast, so all you have to do is start the baking." She held out her empty coffee cup. "Be a sweetie and grab me a refill?"

Lacy reached for the cup. "You've got all the prep work done? What time did you get here?"

"I don't know." She shrugged. "Around five, I guess. I wanted to get at this paperwork. My accountant is breathing down my neck about payroll. The man drives me insane."

Lacy refilled the cup from the urn in the kitchen, added cream and sugar, and set it on her boss' desk before returning to the kitchen to prepare the morning's baked goods. As she worked, she indulged in her favorite daydream. The dreary restaurant kitchen with its antiquated equipment faded away and was replaced by gleaming, state-of-the-art appliances as she stood in her own bakery, creating world-renowned pastries …

At seven forty-five she pulled the last tray of apple turnovers out of the oven and headed to the break room to change. Moments later, Rachel, the breakfast shift waitress, walked in. Her glance swept over Lacy's uniform.

"I thought you were cooking today."

"Change of plans. You'll be covering section two today. I'll take one and three." She shed her jeans and sweater and pulled on the black slacks, red shirt, and white pocket apron that branded her as a Coffee Cup waitress. "Brittany quit yesterday."

"I know."

"You know?"

"She told me she was going to."

"Thanks for the heads-up."

"I didn't want to say anything, you know, in case she changed her mind. But you know that guy she's been seeing, Tyler? He got a good job down south and he asked her to go with him."

"And she pulled up stakes and went. Just like that?"

"Yeah."

Lacy brushed out her hair and pulled it into a tight ponytail. "Smart move," she muttered. In the dining room, she turned on the lights and unlocked the front door while Rachel busied herself with setting out place mats and silverware.

"I'd get out of here in a minute, if some guy invited me to go," Rachel said, her voice tinged with resentment. "But I'd want an engagement ring first."

Lacy snorted. Of that she had no doubt. At nineteen, Rachel was desperate for a home and babies, and didn't seem to care how she got them. The girl fell in love at least once a week.

Silly little fool. As shallow as it sounded, Lacy intended to marry for money, if at all.

"Let me tell you something, friend. An engagement ring is nothing more than a symbol of ownership. Once it's on your finger, you give up the right to make your own decisions."

"Not always," Rachel answered, defensive now. "There are still plenty of good guys out there."

Lacy grabbed up a stack of menus, not answering. When she was Rachel's age, she'd wanted the same things. She'd thought Angel was one of the good guys, had believed in his promises to love and take care of her. She'd thought his money equated to security, and had never thought to question where it came from. In the end, that blind faith had cost her dearly.

She slapped the menus down on the counter. "Whatever, Rachel."

"I'm just saying."

"Go ahead and start another pot of coffee. I'll finish setting up the tables."

At eight o'clock the breakfast customers started straggling in. By nine the tables in her section had turned over twice, and by ten Lacy had already earned forty-three dollars in tips. At ten-thirty, the restaurant started to empty out as the breakfast regulars paid their bills and left. Knowing she had nearly an hour before the local secretaries and bank tellers started arriving for lunch, Lacy grabbed her favorite coffee cup, the blue Superwoman mug Doreen had given her for her birthday the year before.

"It's starting to die down," she told Rachel. "I'm going to go and take my break."

The front door opened and a blast of frigid air whooshed in, followed by a man. His eyes connected with Lacy's for a moment before he grabbed the newspaper from an empty table and sat down at a booth in her section. Despite her resolve, her breath hitched. It was the third day in a row he'd come in. Lacy wasn't usually affected by the men who patronized the diner, but damn. He was the best looking man she'd seen in a long, long time.

This side of thirty, he was tall and blond and totally jacked. But his frayed winter jacket and overgrown hair marked him as a Townie. Maybe not her town, but one just like it. Not the sort of man who could make her dreams come true. In fact, very likely the stuff of nightmares. There was something slightly dangerous about the way he carried himself, something dark and vaguely familiar hiding behind his killer blue eyes. She knew what he was, and he was no one she wanted to get involved with.

Rachel's glance swept over him greedily and Lacy could see the girl was well on her way to falling in love again. "Go ahead and take your break, Lacy. I'll cover your table," she said, already swaying toward him, a come-and-get-me smile painted on her face.

Lacy shook her head. Silly little fool. Pouring the last of the coffee into her mug, she headed out back to take her break.

•

He liked her type. Tall. Dark hair. Large, expressive eyes. Not beautiful, but definitely appealing. Her ice queen expression hinted at a cold heart, but Chase knew better. He knew about her past, her insecurities. He knew a lot of things about Lacy Kennedy that he had no business knowing.

Still, he liked the no-nonsense way she walked and the self-confidence that seemed to pour out of her. He'd noticed it the first time he'd seen her. And every time since. He noticed it now, as she turned and disappeared through the doorway and out of sight. If he didn't know better, Chase would think the lady was avoiding him. It would take some time to break her down. A wry smile played at his mouth. Fine by him. Time was something he had plenty of.

Another waitress appeared. Young. The pretty, needy type. "What can I get you, hon?" she asked.

"Coffee."

"I'm just about to start a fresh pot. Like a little sugar in that, hon?"

"Black."

"You bet."

Three hours earlier, Max had fed him enough breakfast for an army. But his visit to the diner wasn't about food. It was about … what?

Why in the hell was he here?

Opening the discarded newspaper, he began his morning ritual. Flipping to the police log, he skimmed through it. Finding nothing of interest, he moved on to the classified ads. A new one caught his eye and he read it closely, evaluating its pros and cons. Not the perfect job, but maybe it would do for the time being.

The waitress returned with his coffee. He took a swallow of the hot, bitter liquid. He'd had better, but he'd sure had worse.

Tucking the classified section of the paper into his jacket, his gaze swept across the nearly empty dining room, resting again on the doorway the woman had disappeared through. He thought of the mistakes he'd made, mistakes that had brought him to the place where he was today. Two wrongs didn't make a right. But maybe he could make it right enough to satisfy his conscience.

Or maybe he should just leave it alone.

He sipped his coffee, wondering if he should leave or wait it out. Two wrongs might well be the end of him. But the way he saw it, he and the woman had a connection. They'd both made the same mistake. They'd both trusted Angel De la Fuente.

Chapter Three

Across the lake, a chill November wind whispered its secrets, causing the last of the autumn leaves to flutter on the branches of the giant maples. Noticing a splash of brilliant blue against the fresh-fallen snow, Polly Church moved to the kitchen window. Beyond the fence, a pair of bluebirds and their male offspring picked at the berries on the holly bushes she'd planted three summers before. It was the first she'd seen of them in nearly a month. It pleased her that they'd chosen to over-winter at the lake with her, rather than migrate. She smiled, making a mental note to plant more bushes in the spring.

Her eyes were drawn beyond the trees to the wash of sunlight that sparkled on the water. The splendor of it confirmed her belief that Sackett's Harbor was the most beautiful inlet on Shadow Lake. She loved it in summer, when the wild phlox and the honeysuckle vine bejeweled the hillside that sloped gently down to the lake. In autumn, when the maples and the oaks burst forth in breathtaking color. But never more than in winter, when layers of glittering snow enveloped the landscape. Watching the flakes drift lazily from the sky, Polly thought, not for the first time, that it was like living in her own little snow globe.

A sudden movement in the trees drew her gaze sharply to the trail. She squinted hard at the empty pathway, where for a moment she thought she'd seen a man walking. She drew a sharp breath to calm the sudden pounding of her heart. The recent rash of break-ins around the lake had left her feeling on edge. But the robberies had all occurred at night, she reminded herself, not at ten-thirty in the morning. She squinted again at the path, and saw only the shadows of maple trees dancing in the wind.

Hearing footsteps behind her, she turned from the window. Her niece, Wendy, slunk through the doorway, barely dressed in a pair of boys' boxer shorts and a skimpy tank top. The sight of so much bare skin on so chilly a morning gave Polly goose pimples.

"Up so soon?" she asked. The comment reeked of sarcasm, despite Polly's efforts to sound cheerful.

Wendy shrugged and poured herself a cup of coffee. "Why get up? It's not like there's anything to do around here anyway. There might as well have been school today, for all the fun this vacation has been."

Pulling in a breath, Polly struggled to hold her temper. "There's a fresh snowfall out there, and a nice big hill. Why don't you go sledding?"

"Nobody sleds any more, Aunt Polly. People tube at Crystal Mountain. But only the popular kids get to go."

"Last I knew Crystal Mountain was a public facility, open to everyone."

"Oh, Aunt Polly." The girl shot her a look that made her feel a hundred years old. "You don't get it."

Moving to the oven, Polly pulled out a sheet of molasses cookies, her face flushing with heat and anger. The girl was right. She didn't get it and never would; this curious sense of entitlement, this gloom and doom that young people wore like a garment for no discernible reason.

When she was a teenager there was no time for self-absorption. The war was on, and with her two brothers off fighting in Vietnam, it fell to Polly, as the oldest daughter, to help her father run the store. By the time the war ended, Mama was too ill to do much of anything, including raising Polly's sister, Claudia, who was no more than an infant. There was no time for moping about. There was bread to be baked, clothes to be washed and ironed, a baby to tend to.

Polly frowned. She'd done her best with Claudia over the years, stepping in as a parent though she wasn't really much more than a girl herself. She'd helped with her homework and listened to her prayers. She'd taken the child to church every Sunday, for all the good it had done her. Setting the cookies on the counter to cool, Polly's glance slid to Wendy's back as she stalked from the room. Her frown deepened. God help her, she didn't want to raise

Claudia's child.

In a month Wendy would be going to Philadelphia to stay with her friend, Dove Denning, for the Christmas holiday. Taking guilty pleasure in that knowledge, she pulled a second tray of cookies from the oven.

The phone rang, and she set the cookies on the counter and moved to the hallway to answer it. "Hello?"

"Polly? It's Maxine."

"Good morning, Maxine."

"I heard about poor Glenda's fall. How is she doing?"

"They say she has a nasty sprain, but you know Glenda. She'll bounce back."

"I'm sure she will. But in the meantime, would you like me to bring a coffee cake for refreshments for tonight's meeting? It's no bother."

Polly thought of the cookies cooling on her counter, and of the large bowlful of dough still waiting to be baked. She stopped herself from mentioning them to Maxine, knowing her friend had been at loose ends since she became a widow. Now more than ever it was important for Maxine to feel needed. "That would be lovely, Max, if you're sure you can manage it."

"I haven't a thing else to do today," Maxine chirped. "I'll whip one up this morning."

"I must say, you're sounding chipper today."

There was a brief pause, and then, "Oh, Polly, the most wonderful thing has happened. Chase has come home."

The news caught Polly off guard. "Really? I'm surprised. I thought he was happy in New York City."

"He asked me to keep it quiet, but I'm just busting to tell someone and I know I can trust you, Polly. I haven't the vaguest idea why he's home, or even how long he'll stay. But it's just so good to see him, to be able to put my hands on my boy again."

Hanging up the phone a few moments later, Polly felt a stab of envy for the bond Maxine shared with her children. She'd never known that kind of love. She'd never known any kind of love at all. Pushing such gloomy thoughts from her mind, she slid another tray of cookies into the oven and moved back to the window, squinting again at the spot where, only moments before, she could have sworn she'd seen a man walking.

•

Shane was happy for Dusty. Really, he was. Finding love at age forty-five and starting a whole new life, especially with a beauty like Dove Denning was truly remarkable. But he had to admit, losing Dusty on such short notice had really put him and Emma in a bind.

Normally it wouldn't matter in November. The campground was all but deserted from October to May, and he wouldn't have need of a general manager until at least early April. But with Emma's plan to hold a winter carnival in just three weeks' time, he was going to need another pair of hands, and need them soon. He went over his to-do list. Sammy Delaney had agreed to put on a Santa suit for the weekend. What a guy. And yesterday Shane had been able to line up a band for the concert they'd planned for that Saturday. A local bar band called Noise Pollution. It was the best he could do on such short notice. God, he hoped they'd be suitable.

Tomorrow he and Mick would get started on stringing the lights. But the next day Mick would be back in school. He'd need another man, ASAP. Which is why Shane Lucy found himself conducting interviews at one o'clock on the twenty-ninth of November, four days after Thanksgiving.

He sighed and ran a hand back through his hair. With a recession that just wouldn't quit and unemployment higher than it had been since the Great Depression, he'd thought applicants would be pouring out of the woodwork. The lack of candidates was disappointing, to say the least. So far he had only four to choose from. He studied the applications on the desk in front of him.

He didn't need a little old man and his little old wife. He didn't need an unemployed dock worker who looked as though he hadn't bathed in a month. And the last thing he needed was a twenty-year-old with a bad attitude. Simply put, he needed someone he could depend on to do the job, and not one of them so far had fit the bill. So he was right back where he started. In and out of Luckville. He stacked the applications and set them on the corner of his desk, then sat back and rubbed his eyes.

The door opened and Emma breezed in like a breath of fresh air. She set a cup of coffee in front of him. "Any luck?"

"Not so much."

"Oh dear. What about the older couple?"

He took a swallow of coffee. "Who, Mister and Misses Methuselah?"

"I thought they seemed sweet."

"They were. But sweet isn't going to get my campsites cleared this spring, Em. The job involves hard physical labor and I just don't see Mr. and Mrs. Keefer splitting wood and raking leaves."

"There was Mr. Wells," she ventured. "He's younger."

"Whew. I wouldn't want to work down wind of him."

She hid a smile. "Shane, be nice."

"It ain't easy, believe me."

"Well, there's another applicant in the waiting room. He looks like he might be more suited to the job."

"There is?" He shuffled through the meager stack of applications. "I thought Kid Rock was the last one."

"He was. But then this other gentleman showed up right out of the blue."

"Without an appointment?"

"Uh-huh."

"That's pretty nervy."

"I'd say it was pretty amb-bitious."

"Of course you would."

"What does that mean?"

"My Emma, always looking at the positive side of people."

"Is that a bad thing?"

"That, my dear, is one of the things I love most about you." He grabbed her hand and pressed a kiss into her palm.

She smiled. "So should I send him in?"

"Absolutely."

Moments after Emma left the room, a tall, heavily muscled man appeared in the doorway. Shane had always thought of himself as good-sized, but this man made him feel small. He stood, his glance moving over the applicant in swift appraisal. He was in his late twenties, with an air of self-assurance that bordered on arrogance. Not exactly fresh from the barber shop, but a definite improvement over the odoriferous dock worker.

"Shane Lucy?" he said.

"That's me." Shane offered his hand. The man's grip was forceful and confident.

"How's it going? I'm Chase Alexander."

"Have a seat." Shane indicated the empty chair, and when the man was seated across from him, said, "So, Chase. Tell me a little bit about yourself."

He hesitated. "Your ad says you need someone who can perform general maintenance, operate heavy equipment, and oversee the daily operations of the campground. I can do all of those things. That's why I'm here."

"Have you got any managerial experience?"

"You could say that. I know how to organize and prioritize. I'm real good at it, actually."

Shane waited for him to elaborate. He didn't.

"Are you from Lake County?"

"I grew up in Sunset Cove, but I've spent the last few years in Queens."

"New York City?"

"Flushing."

"Where you organized and prioritized ...?"

He hesitated. "I was with the police department. A special D.E.A. task force."

Shane smiled. "I'm afraid you might find your old stomping grounds a bit tamer than what you're used to."

He shrugged. Shane considered the hint of weariness in his eyes, the slightly hollow quality beneath his tough veneer that spoke of sorrow and loss. It was a look he could identify with. One he'd worn himself, not so long ago.

"Are you planning to stay in the area, Chase? I'm looking for someone to fill the position long-term."

"To be honest with you, Shane, I don't have any long-term plans. But I can promise you I'm the best applicant you'll get."

Shane considered the available candidates. Of that he had no doubt. "We're planning a winter carnival for mid-December. Just three weeks from now. Pulling it all together is going to take some doing. I hope you're not afraid to get your hands dirty."

"Not at all."

"Could you give me any references?"

"Maxine Perkins."

"How do you know Maxine?"

"She raised me."

Shane brightened. "You're one of Maxine's boys?"

"That's right."

"That's good enough for me. Maxine Perkins is a saint." Picking up a pencil, he scribbled her name on a notepad. "Why don't you come back in the morning, around nine o'clock. I'll give you a tour of the campground, show you what you'll be doing."

"I'm hired, then?"

Shane nodded and the man's mouth set in a grim line, as though he'd accomplished something unpleasant but necessary.

"Then I guess I'll see you tomorrow."

When he'd ambled from the room, Emma slipped back inside, her eyebrows raised in question.

"I have to make a phone call," Shane told her. "But if his reference checks out, it looks like we may have found our guy."

•

Later that evening Lacy once again stood in front of the abandoned bakery, her hands shoved deep inside her pockets. It was after six o'clock and the winter sky was dark with clouds. She'd stayed through the second shift after Doreen finally gave in to her migraine and went home. It had been a long, backbreaking day and Lacy was exhausted to her bones.

Reflected in the window, the garish blue lights of a fiber-optic Christmas tree winked from inside the Laundromat across the street. A rush of warmth spread through her as she thought of the twinkling white lights and red velvet bows that would decorate the windows of her bakery some day. It would happen. She'd come too far to stop believing it now.

All at once, the impending end of another year made her feel nostalgic. Memories flooded over her and she saw her childhood as clearly as if the bakery window were a window to her past. She was transfixed, transported back in time to when she was eight years old, to when the dream began. When, like a hummingbird, unaware of its role as pollinator as it extracts nectar from a flower and then flits to another, perpetuating the species, so Gretchen Kruger had unwittingly transferred her dream of becoming a pastry chef to Lacy Kennedy.

Back then, most people looked at Lacy and saw a tough-talking little girl with ragged fingernails and crookedly cut hair. Beyond help, her teachers agreed, both academically and socially. Little did they know her sassiness was a cover-up for the aching loneliness she felt. That her unwillingness to try their math problems and spelling words stemmed from a deep seated fear of getting it wrong, of being rejected.

Lost and lonely, Lacy spent her days sitting alone on the fire escape, taking pleasure in the pigeons that roosted in the eaves of the abandoned factory across the street. At night, she'd lie in bed and listen to the radio, dreaming of having a better life; a pretty house, a mother who wasn't so tired. Of having a friend. She'd feel the stabs of pain that came with knowing that none of those dreams would ever be fulfilled, and she'd bury her face in her pillow and cry the silent tears of an outcast. Such was the way of life for Lacy Kennedy. Until the summer the Krugers moved in to the apartment upstairs.

On that sweltering Sunday morning, Lacy crouched on the fire escape, watching in fascination as a woman and a girl unloaded boxes from the back of a U-Haul trailer. The woman was enormous, with a purple flowered tent dress and a pair of thick, silver ropes curling like sausages around her head. The girl was about Lacy's size, with golden hair and a matched set of dimples on either side of her pretty mouth. Lacy would spend the rest of the summer poking the eraser end of a pencil into her cheeks, trying in vain to recreate those captivating divots on her own face.

As she hauled the last box from the back of the trailer, the woman stopped and placed her large hands on the small of her back. In mid-massage, she glanced upward. Spying Lacy on the fire escape, her mouth stretched into a wide smile. "Yoo-hoo! Good day, Madchen!" she called, excitedly flapping her hands. Her words were encased in a thick accent Lacy didn't recognize. "You and my Valerie will be nice, good friends, I think. Come upstairs later and have some kuchen with us, ya?"

Startled, Lacy scampered back inside, not answering.

But later that afternoon, drawn by curiosity, she stood with her ear pressed tight to the door of the woman's apartment. The heavenly scent of apples and cinnamon drifted into the hallway, making her mouth water. She was agonizing over whether or not to knock when the door swung open and all at once she was face to face with the tent dress woman.

Up close, Lacy could see that her eyes were of the palest blue, kind eyes that seemed to see the very secrets of her heart. "So you did come back, Madchen," she said gently. "Please, come inside. Valerie's been waiting for you."

"Thank you, Ma'am," Lacy said, averting her gaze.

"You may call me Gretchen."

There were boxes stacked in every inch of the Kruger's apartment, but Gretchen had unpacked the necessities, the things she said made a house *heimisch*—a home. There were small figurines she called Hummels, bright purple and gold afghans, beautiful paintings of forests and rivers; things it wouldn't even occur to Lacy's mother to own. She stared in wonder at a glass-fronted cabinet, its legs carved with gnomes and cherubs, and tried to imagine owning such a wonderful piece of furniture.

Unlike Lacy, who'd grown up fatherless and impoverished, Valerie had known the comfort of a two-parent home. Her father had died three years earlier, in an accident on the loading docks at the boat yard, where he'd worked for thirty years. His life insurance policy left his wife and daughter enough money to live on, if they were careful, but eventually, Gretchen had been forced to sell their home in Dutch Landing and move into the apartment in the alley behind Arbor Street. Strange, Lacy would later think, that the Kruger's misfortune could bring about such a wondrous turn of events for her. That afternoon in Gretchen Kruger's apartment marked the beginning of the most incredible chapter of Lacy's life.

That summer was a magical time of friendship; of swimming and of sand castles and of dreams. Lacy showed Valerie how to climb the rungs to the top of Townline Bridge, where you could see clear across the lake. She showed her the places where the rock doves roosted, and taught her how to make a collage from the soft, blue gray feathers they shed. When September rolled around, Lacy didn't dread school as much as she normally would, knowing that for the first time ever, she'd have a friend to sit with on the bus.

On the first morning of school, Lacy arrived at the Kruger's apartment to find Valerie scrubbed pink and dressed in a red and blue plaid skirt, its pleats ironed into perfect creases. Her blonde hair was plaited into two shiny braids. They hung to her shoulders, the ends punctuated by blue velveteen ribbons. Dressed in a rumpled cotton skirt, Lacy felt shabby by comparison.

"Sit," Gretchen commanded. When Lacy complied, the older woman combed the snarls from her hair and pulled it into braids, affixing little pink bows to ends. Finished, she smiled. "Look at my pretty little *Schulerinnen*, my little school girls." But hidden just beneath the surface of Gretchen's smile, Lacy saw trepidation. She wondered if it had to do with Valerie's learning disability.

Valerie had told her she had something called dyslexia. When she tried to read, the letters jumbled around like alphabet soup in her head. The other children had teased her mercilessly and finally Gretchen had taken Valerie out of school and hired a private tutor. No longer able to afford that luxury, Gretchen had had to enroll Valerie at Hope Haven Elementary School. Valerie was small for her age, but Gretchen assured her she would fit in beautifully with the other third graders, despite the fact that she was three years older.

In spite of her pretty smile and perfectly plaited hair, Valerie's mended clothes and her alliance with Lacy quickly branded her as an outcast. As they walked through the double doors of the elementary school, Lacy averted her gaze from the popular girls in their pretty, new clothes. "Hey, look at the new girl," a beauty named Stacy Standish said, a nasty look on her face.

"Nice outfit," her friend, Rita Mark, chimed in. "I think I saw that this summer on the mannequin in the window at the Salvation Army Thrift Store."

The girls erupted into giggles, causing Lacy's hands to ball into fists.

"She stinks!" Stacy sidled up to Valerie, taking a theatrical sniff. "She smells like a dirty old dish rag."

Just as a fresh round of giggles erupted, Lacy's fist connected with Stacy's nose, sending a pool of blood splashing down on Stacy's pretty, new dress, and Lacy spent her first day of the third grade sitting in the principal's office.

The other girls might have eventually forgiven Valerie for being poor, due to the fact that she was the prettiest girl in class. But the kiss of death for any chance Valerie might have had at acceptance came on the fourth of October, the day Gretchen showed up at the school with a basket of treats for Valerie's eleventh birthday.

"She's eleven years old," the other girls whispered. "Eleven years old and still in the third grade?"

Whispers rippled across the classroom like waves across a pond.

"She must be a moron!"

"Yes, a moron. And did you get a look at her mother?"

From that day on, Valerie apologized for Gretchen's enormous size and her thick German accent, like they were something to be ashamed of, but Lacy thought Gretchen was wonderful. Her life was all about giving and laughter. She was the polar opposite of Lacy's own mother, whose life was about working and finding a husband. In that order. Sometimes she'd be gone for days at a time, leaving Lacy alone or with whoever would take her. And more often than not, the taker was Gretchen Kruger.

On Saturday mornings, after she'd prepared Valerie's and Lacy's breakfast, Gretchen would tie on her white apron and get busy making pastries and pies which she'd sell in the farmer's market for extra cash. Lacy would watch, fascinated, as Gretchen's work-roughened hands blended sugar and flour, as they rolled out papery thin pastry crust.

One morning Gretchen gave Lacy an apron and set her up at the table with a rolling pin and a batch of dough. Despite her best efforts, the dough stuck to the pin. The harder Lacy tried to duplicate Gretchen's masterpiece, the worse the dough looked. Finally she threw it down in frustration. "I can't do it," she cried, tears welling in her eyes.

Gretchen retrieved the doughy mess, and working her magic, pieced it back together. "There now. It's not so bad," she said gently. "You see?"

"How do you do it, Gretchen? How do you make it look so pretty?"

"The secret is the love." She planted a kiss on Lacy's forehead. "Some day, Madchen, you will make pretty pastries too. I can feel the love right here, in your hands."

Soon the tantalizing scent of their labors filled the small apartment. To Lacy, Gretchen's pastries represented happiness, and she felt as if every good thing in the world were wrapped up inside them.

The Kruger's moved away when Lacy was thirteen, but the dream lived on. By then, it was so deeply rooted inside of Lacy she couldn't remember a time she hadn't wanted it. Deprived of the comfort of Gretchen's sunny kitchen, she practiced her baking in her mother's cramped, messy kitchenette instead.

A year after Valerie and Grechen moved away, Lacy's mother finally got her husband; a drunken slob named Doc who made Lacy's life unbearable. He spent his days barking orders, or worse, passed out on the couch. On those days, Lacy was forbidden to work in the kitchen, or to make any noise at all. Two years later, when the beatings started, Lacy fled her mother's home and moved in with Angel De la Fuente, inadvertently jumping from the fry pan straight into the fires of hell.

The chill evening air cut through her jacket like a knife, scattering her memories. As Lacy turned to leave, she saw another image reflected in the window behind her. The image of a car. It cruised by slowly, a battered blue Chevy with a dented fender. She recognized it immediately. She'd seen it nearly every day that week, parked in front of the Coffee Cup. It was the blond stranger's car.

The Chevy idled a block away, its motor revving. Lacy shivered with fear. She wanted to run, but her legs felt heavy and dead. As the car crawled forward again, she forced herself to put one foot in front of the other. She told herself it was a coincidence, him being in her neighborhood, that it had nothing to do with her at all. But another part of her didn't believe it. Not for a moment. Irrational fear crept over her, making her scalp tingle and her heart flutter. She told herself she was being silly. She'd done nothing wrong. But a small inner voice whispered that it didn't always matter. She'd become familiar with injustice at a young age. So many warm summer nights she'd stood in the alley, watching as Sunset Cove boys were thrown into the back seats of police cars and hauled downtown for questioning. Their only crime, living on the wrong side of town.

At the light, the car hesitated. Lacy held her breath until finally it turned right and disappeared around the corner. She shuddered, concentrated on putting one foot in front of the other. Living with Angel all those years, she'd become street savvy. His criminal instinct had honed hers to a razor's edge. Four years after his arrest, the uncanny intuition remained. The uncomfortable prickling at the base of her scalp that told her the handsome stranger was a cop.

Chapter Four

At seven o'clock that evening, Polly Church's glance skimmed over the meeting room. All of the usual members were in attendance, as well as a few new faces she didn't recognize. It was remarkable, she thought, how much the group had grown in five short years. The Sialia Society had started with three members who'd met in Polly's living room on the first Monday of each month to discuss bluebirds. A year later, ten members had started bluebird trails. As their numbers continued to swell and their Monday night projects became more involved, Polly had secured a grant from the local Ornithology Society and was able to rent an empty studio apartment on Heron Street; twelve hundred square feet of meeting space with a kitchen as an added bonus. And now the group was outgrowing that.

She considered the rows of folding chairs, all of them filled. Thankfully Sammy Delaney had had the foresight to borrow a dozen chairs from the church hall that afternoon. He'd even met her there an hour before the meeting to help set up, God love him. Her gaze moved to the kitchen, where they'd set up work stations with lard, peanut butter, and rolled oats. Later tonight the group would be making suet.

Satisfied that all was in good order, her glance moved down the agenda for that night's meeting. After a brief word of welcome, she'd go over the minutes from last month's meeting, and then she'd give the presentation. A slide show. She hoped it would go off without any sort of hitch. God knew she was no kind of technological wizard.

Wendy had put the show together for her, had created a masterpiece from the menagerie of photos the members had sent in. Lovely photos of bluebird eggs and nesting females, photos of proud orioles and flaming red cardinals and sweet hummingbirds, their tiny wings aflutter. Best of all were the shots of the fledglings. Wendy had even thought to add music.

Polly's smile dipped into a frown. She'd counted on the girl coming tonight to run the computer for them, but at the last moment Wendy said she wasn't feeling well. She'd explained to Polly how to start the program and how to project the image from the laptop onto the oversized screen. She'd even written it all down for her, step by step. Polly sighed. Sammy had assured her that all would go well. Even so, she'd feel better if Wendy was here to oversee things.

•

As soon as her Aunt's car pulled out of the driveway, Wendy sprung into action. Grabbing up her cell phone, she sent Cassidy a text.

She's gone.

She held her breath as she waited for Cassidy's reply.

Bout dam time. U gd 2 go?

Give me 10.

5!

Stripping off her joggers and camisole, she tossed them on the bed, then pulled on her favorite black jeans and her black Noise Pollution T-shirt. She rooted through her jewelry box and pulled out her ear gauges and the silver stud Aunt Polly made her take out of her cheek when she moved in with her the summer before, saying that piercings were in poor taste for a young lady.

Putting in the gauges wasn't a problem. Wendy had secretly worn them to bed every night for weeks to keep the holes from closing up. The stud was another matter. She winced at the stinging sensation as she pushed it through the hole in her cheek. A pinprick of blood formed and she wiped it away with a tissue, persevering until at last the stud poked through.

Her jewelry in place, she applied eye shadow, liner and a heavy coat of mascara, then brushed her long, jet-black hair, carefully arranging it so it partially concealed her left eye. Standing back, she studied her reflection. She wasn't entirely satisfied with her look, but there was no time to fix it. Out front, Cassidy was leaning on the horn. Her stomach filled with dizzy butterflies, Wendy bolted down the stairs and out the front door, slamming it behind her as she hurried out into the night.

Cassidy pulled away before Wendy could even buckle her seatbelt. "What the hell took so long? I thought you said she was leaving at six."

"I had to show her a hundred times how to run the slide show." She dug in her purse for a cigarette. "She's totally hopeless. Let me use your lighter, will you?"

Cassidy handed over her Zippo, glancing at Wendy's bare arms. "You're going to freeze, you know. The warehouse isn't heated."

Wendy lit her cigarette, the cold already biting through her thin tee shirt. She shrugged. So she'd be cold. Who cared? She would have gone to hear Noise Pollution practice if it had been thirty below zero. They were her favorite local band and she had to let Brandon Blake see what a die-hard fan she was.

She'd first heard Noise Pollution play at a free concert in Windham Park last summer. They'd blown her away. The deep, driving rhythms of Bogey's guitar and the heartbeat of Quinn's drums was intoxicating. But it was the lead singer, Brandon Blake, who mesmerized her. His voice, low, smooth and smoky, took her to another place, providing the escape she so desperately needed. It didn't hurt that Brandon was cute beyond belief, with blue eyes, tight jeans, and tons of bad-ass tattoos covering his arms. She'd hung around for hours after the concert, waiting for a chance to talk to him with no such luck. And then, last month, when her golden opportunity landed in her lap, she'd straight up blown it. If she could just have another chance to talk to him, to tell him how much his music meant to her, she wouldn't wreck it this time by acting like a star-struck fool.

She inhaled deeply on her cigarette, coughed, and threw it out the window. Her thoughts drifted back to the homecoming dance and she cringed. Fool! But then, feeling like a fool was nothing new to her.

It had been hard, changing her whole life. When her mother went to jail she had to move away from her home in Union City and live with Aunt Polly in the small, quiet lake community. She'd had a tough time fitting in. Brandon's music made her feel like there was someone on the planet understood her pain. His music made her miserable life almost bearable.

Her thoughts bridged to Mick Lucy. He was the first person who'd even bothered to speak to her in school. At first she'd dared to hope that Mick liked her as more than a friend, but then she realized she was nothing special to him. Mick was nice to everyone. They'd kissed a couple of times, but nothing ever came of it and Wendy got tired of waiting. He didn't like Noise Pollution and he made it pretty clear he didn't like the crowd she was hanging out with now. Which is his problem, not mine, she thought, pushing all thoughts of Mick from her mind.

When they reached the city limits, Cassidy maneuvered through a maze of streets and back alleys and finally pulled into a parking lot across from a creepy looking brick building. Its upstairs windows seemed to stare at her like accusing eyes and she shivered again. It was as if the building knew she was doing something she shouldn't be. Or maybe it was just her guilty conscience.

"You ready?" Cass asked, impatience tinting the edges of her voice.

Wendy's glance swept over the parking lot. It was empty except for a pair of beat-up F-150s and a totally trashed mini van. "Doesn't look like anyone's around," Wendy said.

"Most of the people who hang here don't have cars." Cassidy pulled a brush through her tangled red-brown curls. "But there's Brandon's truck."

Wendy eyed the derelict vehicles, a secret thrill passing through her.

"Which one?"

"The red one."

"Really?"

"Yeah. And don't go getting all geeky on me."

"What's that supposed to mean?"

"It means don't act like some giggling little fool."

Wendy's face burned with shame as she thought again of last month's fiasco, when Noise Pollution had played at the Homecoming dance at her school. She'd taken her notepad full of songs, determined to show them to Brandon. Afterward, she'd finally gotten a chance to meet him and she'd blown it, big time. She and some of her friends had smuggled a six-pack of beer into the dance, and by the time Cass' boyfriend had introduced her to Brandon, Wendy had been too drunk to do more than giggle like a flaming idiot. But that wouldn't happen this time. This was her last chance. She wouldn't blow it again.

Third time's a charm, she reminded herself.

As Cassidy cut the engine and threw open her door, the muffled sounds of heavy metal music drifted to Wendy across the frigid air. Her heart fluttered in her chest and she caught herself wanting to pinch her arm to make sure the moment was real, that she was really getting another chance to meet Brandon Blake.

Cassidy was evening the score by bringing her here, she knew. Cass' brother, Quinn, had recently joined up as Noise Pollution's drummer after Billy the Equalizer went into rehab for his alcohol addiction and now Cass got to go and hear the band practice every night. As luck would have it, Cass owed Wendy a favor. Wendy had been supplying the booze for Cass' Friday night parties for a month from the stash of homemade wine and blackberry brandy Aunt Polly kept in the cellar. When the pinpricks of guilt came, she told herself it wasn't stealing, exactly. More like extra payment for the dusting and vacuuming and all the other junk Aunt Polly was always making her do. And anyway, Aunt Polly had more than enough wine for one old lady. With her arthritis acting up, she never went down cellar anyway. She'd never miss a few lousy bottles.

But after tonight, she and Cass would be squared up. After tonight, as far as Brandon was concerned, she was on her own.

Walking toward the warehouse, her skin prickled with cold and excitement. Her notepad felt like a twenty-pound weight in her back pocket.

"Just remember," Cassidy warned, "Keep your mouth shut around Brandon."

"I will," Wendy said. She surreptitiously crossed her fingers in her pockets, because no way was she going to keep that promise.

Inside, the music was deafening. Through a haze of cigarette smoke, Wendy could make out a crush of people laughing and hanging out. They were crowded around the band, making it tough for her to get a good look at Brandon. But just knowing she was in the same room with him made her feel light-headed. While Cassidy ambled to the corner where her boyfriend, Cal, smoked a cigarette and swigged a bottle of Power Ade, Wendy turned and strode across the room to where the band was playing.

•

So far the meeting was going smoothly. Polly had welcomed the group, reminding the guests to fill out new membership forms. If all of them joined, it would bring their enrollment up to thirty-six. She'd read the minutes from last month's meeting, talked about the bird feeder project that would be starting the next week, and passed out tip sheets for over-wintering bluebirds.

"A little bit later you'll each get a chance to make a batch of suet to take home with you," she announced, "But first, I've prepared a special surprise. Sam?"

On cue, Sammy Delaney switched off the lights, and Polly booted up the computer, praying that the only surprises would be pleasant ones. She sighed with relief as the soft strains of classical music floated across the air and lovely images filled the screen at the front of the room. Some were Polly's own photos; a male bluebird feeding his offspring, a downy woodpecker perching on the shed roof, a sleek waxwing singing from the foliage of an evergreen. Next came the photos the members had sent to her, photos of robin's eggs, a chimney swift, and a pair of swallows. Some were badly out of focus, but others were quite lovely. In all, the presentation went off like a dream and Polly silently thanked the good Lord and her niece's creativity.

After a burst of applause, Polly called the meeting back to order. "Mr. Delaney and I have prepared work stations in the kitchen area. You'll find everything you need to make your own batch of suet. Are there any questions before we get started?"

Maxine Perkins' hand shot up. "As you know, Polly, I've made suet before, but I can't seem to get the bluebirds to eat it."

Polly noticed how pretty Maxine looked. The crimson shawl and navy pants suit she wore brought out the radiance in her skin. Her eyes positively sparkled with a happiness that had been lacking since she lost her husband, Willy. Polly knew the reason for the transformation. The joy of Chase's homecoming. The power of love. She felt another pinprick of envy and quickly pushed it aside.

"I have a different problem," Ginny Watkins chimed in. Polly winced inwardly, seeing the scowl on the woman's face. Why was it that Ginny always had to add her two dirty pennies to every conversation?

"Before the bluebirds have a chance at my suet, the squirrels eat my feeder out of house and home," Ginny complained. "I finally gave up on the birds and just let the furry buggers have at it."

"Those aren't uncommon problems, ladies," Polly assured them. "Bluebirds have to be trained to eat from a feeder. And there are ways to dissuade unwanted dinner guests, like squirrels. We'll discuss that a little bit later in the project, as well as what types of feeders to put out to attract bluebirds."

"I have worlds of leftover scrap wood in my shop, and boxes full of patterns. If anyone would like to come over sometime, I'd be glad to help them build one." The offer came from Sammy and Polly smiled at him. Such a kind and generous man, she thought. Always the first to offer help.

"Thank you, Sam. That was a lovely offer and I'm sure several of our members will take you up on it. Now, if everyone's ready, let's go out to the kitchen and we'll get started."

•

At seven-fifteen, Chase sat in his car a block from Lacy's apartment building, his engine idling. He took a bite of his greasy hamburger, his eyes trained on her front door. What kind of fool was he?

Earlier, Max had told him she was going out for the evening, and had offered to make his dinner before she left. There was no point in putting her to the trouble, so he decided to go back to the diner on the off chance that Lacy would still be there. He'd have a bite to eat. And then he'd spill his guts.

The dinner shift waitress said he'd missed her by minutes. Cruising slowly down Arbor Street, he'd caught sight of a fawn colored jacket, a tangle of dark hair and his heart started racing. Lacy stood, staring into the window of an abandoned building. It was the perfect opportunity to talk with her, and yet he sat, torn with indecision, revving his engine like a fool and probably scaring her senseless. Outstanding move, Alexander. He'd always prided himself on his impeccable sense of timing, but when it came to Lacy Kennedy he felt like a bumbling idiot.

He choked down the last bite of his burger and threw the wrapper in the back seat. He turned up the heat, and he thought about tigers and buttercups. His memories took on a life of their own, and he heard the echo of Angel's voice as clearly as if he sat in the car beside him.

"I shouldn't have freaked out on her like that, ya know? She only did it to make me happy."

It was a warm summer night, and they sat on the hood of Chase's car, drinking beer and talking about regrets. Angel had been telling Chase about his and Lacy's first place. About how Lacy had taken a class in stenciling and had come home and painted buttercups on the bedroom walls.

"It was a freaking mess, you know? She had these blobs of paint everywhere, but she was so excited to show me what she'd done. She was trying to make the house a home. And I screamed at her for it. I wish I hadn't done that …"

As Angel spoke, a memory hit Chase like a fist in the gut. A long-buried memory of his life before Sunset Cove. A memory of his mother. As a child he'd been fascinated by tigers, and as a surprise birthday gift, his mother had painted a parade of them across his bedroom wall. He'd been mesmerized by their golden eyes and their long, striped tails. He couldn't have been more than three or four, but he remembered with crystal clarity the joy of those tigers, and the sheer terror of his father's wrath.

He'd come home from work that night and screamed at Chase's mother, shouting about how she'd ruined the apartment. The next day he'd bought a can of white paint and erased the tigers, one by one, while Chase stood crying.

"Please don't do this, Jack," his mother pleaded. "They're not hurting anything."

"They're stupid!" his father yelled. "They're the stupidest damn things I've ever seen. Except for you."

"They made him happy. What's so wrong with that?"

The memory faded away, leaving Chase shaken.

That night, on the hood of Chase's car, Angel painted a picture that made Lacy come alive for Chase. A picture that made him fall in love with her. As the weeks passed, Angel talked about Lacy constantly, and the more he talked, the more Chase wanted her. It wasn't that he was trying to replace his long-lost mother, but he wanted the kind of woman who would paint buttercups on the bedroom wall. The kind of woman that baked cupcakes on cloudy days and frosted them with all the colors of the rainbow. A woman who filled the house with laughter and vases of dandelions. A woman like Lacy Kennedy.

He stared at the door of her apartment, as if the sheer force of his will would make her materialize. He kicked the heat up another notch. He was weary of the burden of his guilt. There were things he needed to tell her. Things she needed to know. She had to come out, sooner or later. He'd wait all night, if that's what it took.

•

Being close to Brandon was a total thrill and Wendy never wanted the evening to end. The night was turning out to be perfect. Sitting with Brandon was intoxicating beyond her wildest dreams. Or maybe it was the can of beer she and Cass had shared. Or a little bit of both. Her eyes slid to Brandon's muscled arm, so close to her own. Was he really sitting right here, near enough to touch? Was he really smiling at her?

God! She hoped she wasn't babbling, telling him about her mother, her school, Aunt Polly and her bluebirds, of all things. But Lord help her, she couldn't seem to keep quiet.

What seemed all too soon, he stubbed out his cigarette on the heel of his boot and stood. "It's been great talking to you, sweetheart, but I've got to get back to work."

"Wait. I … I've got something to show you." Before she could chicken out, she fumbled the notepad from her pocket and thrust it into his hands. "These are some songs I wrote. They're probably not very good."

"Yeah, okay. I'll look at them later, if I get a chance." Jamming the notepad in the pocket of his jeans, he turned and strode away. She watched, breathless, as he walked back to the platform and grabbed up his guitar. It took her a few moments to realize the delicious buzzing sensation was coming, not from inside her, but from her cell phone. Flipping it open, she was annoyed to see Aunt Polly's cell number displayed on her screen. What did she want now? She angrily pushed her hair out of her eyes, wishing she'd never encouraged her aunt to get a cell phone, wishing she'd never taught her how to use one. As Brandon and the band went back to their practicing, Wendy slipped out the front door and around the side of the building to return the call.

•

"You sit down, Polly. I can get that."

Polly sank into a nearby chair, shooting Sammy a grateful look as he began cleaning up the kitchen. All things considered, the evening had gone beautifully. Thirty-six batches of suet had gone out tonight. The area bluebirds would eat well this month, and Polly found that personally gratifying. Even so, the evening had taken its toll. She was weary right down to her toes. "Thanks for your help, Sam," she said.

"It's my pleasure."

They chatted about the meeting as Sammy cleaned up the work stations and stowed the last of the supplies in the pantry. When he'd finished, he extended his hands and helped her to her feet.

"Would you like to go out for a cup of coffee, Polly? I know of a great little café over on the Boulevard that's open all night. They make a mighty nice cappuccino."

A warm glow started in Polly's middle and slowly spread through her. She would have loved nothing more than to enjoy a cup of coffee with Sam Delaney. Still, she told herself, there was little point in it.

"I'd like that, Sam. But I should go home and check on Wendy. She wasn't feeling well this evening, and as usual, she's not answering her cell phone."

"If she isn't feeling well, then she's probably sound asleep."

He had a point, and he looked so eager that Polly felt herself soften. He was such a sweet man. And it had been so long since she'd enjoyed a man's company. Longer than she could remember.

"Well, I suppose a half hour wouldn't make so much of a difference."

His face broke into a boyish grin, though Sammy was well into his sixth decade, the same as her. "Well, then. Shall we?"

After a brisk walk to his car, Polly settled into the front seat.

Sammy started the engine, and within moments heat began to radiate from the seat beneath her. Polly had never owned anything more luxurious than her sturdy, ten-year-old pickup truck. She marveled at the wonder of Sammy's luxury sedan, with its heated seats and its sophisticated stereo system. Within moments their companionable silence was broken by the soft chirp of her cell phone.

Flipping it open, she squinted at the screen. "It's my niece calling," she announced. "Hello?"

"Did you call me, Aunt Polly?" Wendy demanded.

"Yes. I called to see how you were feeling."

"I'm fine." Her irritation seeped through the phone, like a wet blanket thrown across Polly's happiness. "I was sleeping."

"I can't imagine how you could sleep, with that racket going on. You're not having a party, are you?"

"No, Aunt Polly. I'm not having a party. That's just my CD player."

"Oh. Well I wanted to let you know that I'm going out for coffee with one of the members of my group." She checked her watch. It was barely nine. "If there's nothing you need, then I should be home no later than ten."

"Okay, Aunt Polly. See you later. I'm going back to sleep now."

"Everything all right?" Sammy asked, as she replaced the phone in her purse.

"Yes. She was resting, just as you said she'd be."

He reached across the seat and patted her hand. Polly gazed out at the snow, which fell against the windshield in light, swirling patterns. In the last couple of years she'd come to dread driving in the winter. It was nice to sit back and leave the bother to someone else. Her gaze shifted to Sammy's large, capable hands as they rested on the steering wheel. Such nice hands. Gentle, yet strong.

Sammy parked the car a block from Rosie's Cafe and held her arm as they walked along the snowy street. The warmth spread through her again and she scolded herself for acting the fool.

Inside, Rosie's was a cozy combination of warm autumn colors and the heavenly scents of exotic coffees. Christmas music spilled softly from a hidden stereo system. Sammy guided her to a corner booth with an oversized window that overlooked the street. She gazed out at what looked like a Currier and Ives painting with twinkling Christmas lights and shimmering angels. Before long a waitress appeared and Sammy ordered two Vanilla Spice cappuccinos and an order of buttered scones.

"Thank you for coming out with me tonight, Polly," Sammy said.

"Why, thank you for inviting me." She removed a napkin from the table and placed it in her lap.

"It's the least I could do." His hand crept across the table and covered hers. "I can't tell you how much it means to me, being a part of the Sialia Society."

"But I'm the one who should be thanking you. All the extra

time you put in, helping to set up, and tear down ..." Flustered, she removed her hand from his and patted her hair into place.

He shrugged. "It gives me something to do. I'll be honest, Polly. At first I only attended the meetings for an evening out. The house has been so empty, since Mary's been gone. But the society has opened my eyes to the joy of birds, the joy of life, again."

Polly smiled gently. "I've had a love affair with birds for more than four decades. It seems the hardest times in my life, the times of greatest stress, have been the times birds have brought me the most joy. That's why I started the society. To help others find that same joy."

Her face grew warm and she looked away, embarrassed at having spoken so freely. Sammy gave her hand a squeeze, drawing her gaze back to his eyes. She saw something kind and wise in them that made her feel accepted, unashamed. She'd known Sammy since grammar school, had even dated him briefly in high school. He was the first boy she'd kissed. But she'd never really felt she knew him until that moment.

She marveled at how different two men could be. Benny had never understood her love of birds, her absolute need to surround herself with them. When they'd first married, she'd hung a feeder outside her kitchen window. With so little money to live on in those days, Benny had belittled her hobby, had begrudged her the little bit of spare change she spent on bird seed. But she'd adored the colorful woodpeckers and grosbeaks, the sweet finches and the cardinals that came to sample her offerings throughout the day. Their cheerful songs and lovely colors infused so much happiness into life that she took Benny's criticism in stride, thinking it a small price to pay for the joy of having birds nearby.

Her love of the bluebird didn't come until years later, when she'd suffered her first bout of cancer. She'd been housebound that spring, undergoing radiation treatments, when out her window she'd caught sight of a female bird building a nest in a rotted fence post. Charmed by the bird's relentless energy and intrigued by her pale gray feathers and russet breast, she'd asked Benny to bring her a bird book from the local library. Within its pages she'd been able to identify the specimen as a female eastern bluebird. Sialia Sialis.

All that spring she'd watched as the female and her lovely mate of vivid blue carried food to their babies. The book had said that bluebirds represented happiness, and that was certainly true. They'd brought her joy during her time of deepest darkness. They'd given her a reason to get up each morning.

Since that time, she'd thought of the birds as her protectors, firmly believing they'd brought about her full recovery. She promised herself that somehow, some day, she'd find a way to repay their kindness. It was more than forty years before she was able to make good on that promise.

"A penny for your thoughts," Sammy said, bringing her back to the present.

The waitress had appeared with their order. "My, my, don't these scones look delicious," she said, retrieving one from the plate.

As if sensing her discomfort, Sammy steered the conversation toward politics. Polly sat back and enjoyed the delicious confection, the warmth and cheerfulness of the café, and the sound of Sammy's voice. A former high school history teacher, Sammy was intensely interested in current events. He liked to parallel history with modern life, pointing out the similarities.

"... So you see, we've had immigration problems throughout history. In the 1920s people thought the solution was to close the doors, as they say, but then, look what happened. Our economy collapsed."

"But surely something must be done."

"Something, yes. But not eradication. History has proven that."

Sammy was a firm believer that those who do not learn from history's mistakes are doomed to repeat them.

She thought about the easy conversation that had always been between them. They'd gone to movies and school dances together what now seemed a century ago. Years before, before he went away to fight in the Vietnam War, overcome with fear and the dread of the unknown, Sammy had asked her to marry him. She couldn't help wondering how different her life would have been if she'd said yes.

•

Wendy was standing off to the side of the warehouse, loving the sound of Brandon's voice and the way he seemed to be singing just for her.

I can't even sleep
I'm constantly at war

When will this cease?
Baby I'm not sure
I'm at war.
Every time you step out
Always shootin' me down
I can't protect myself
On this battlefield
I need help
So rescue me now, babe.
Rescue me now.

Was it possible? Did Brandon feel vulnerable and afraid, just like her? He must, or how could he write these songs? She closed her eyes, letting his words sink into her soul.

On this battlefield, I'm deserted
With no tanks or bombs
I'm worthless, useless
To come along and blow me up,
That's what you did, baby
U invaded my territory
The space was great
That we could'a shared
But you had a different story
U played along with me
Put me on the front line
With a banner spellin' el-oh-ve-ee
I was sickened by the motion
Of this whole other scene
I wasn't equipped for. My legs were sore
From running back and forth
From your bunk to my bunk
but the enemy in this one …
In this one, it was you, hon.

Shivers raced across her heart, because in his words, she found solace. She wasn't alone. Brandon, too, knew about betrayal.

All at once Cassidy's words broke the magic spell. "Time's up, Cinderella."

"Let's stay just a few more minutes."

Cassidy shrugged. "It doesn't matter to me, girlfriend. But it's getting late. You said your aunt would be home at ten. If we leave right now, we can be back before she is. That's if we leave right now."

With a last, longing glance at Brandon, Wendy turned and followed her friend, closing the door on Brandon's soulful wailing.

"Man, it's cold," she complained, hurrying across the lot.

"I told you to wear a hoodie." They'd reached the car, and Cassidy jammed the key in the ignition and turned the heat up full throttle. Cold air blasted from the vents, taking Wendy's breath away.

"So?" Cass said.

"So, what?"

"So did you have fun?"

Wendy shrugged. "It was all right."

"What were you and Brandon talking about earlier?"

Wendy shrugged again. "Nothing much."

Cassidy chuckled. "Must have been pretty good. You looked as happy as a pig in a big ol' pile of slop."

Despite Cassidy's unflattering simile, Wendy glowed inside. She played her conversation with Brandon over and over in her head as they rushed through the city and out of town, as they cruised up the winding road that led to Shadow Lake. But when they pulled onto October Lane and the headlights swept across Aunt Polly's house, the glow disappeared and an icy fist clenched her insides.

"Dude, you left the front door open?" Cassidy's glance moved from Wendy to the door.

"No. I know I closed it behind me." She stared at the open door, suddenly filled with fear.

"Then how did it get open? Man, that house is going to be like an icebox."

Wendy's worried glance moved over the house, pausing at each window. "Do you think someone's in there?"

"God, I didn't think of that. I hope not."

"Will you come in with me? Just for a minute?"

Cassidy lost her breath. "I told Cal I'd be right back."

"Please?"

Cass lost her breath again and Wendy couldn't tell if it was from fear or annoyance. "All right. But just for a minute."

As she tiptoed up the walkway, Wendy noticed two sets of footprints leading away from the house. "Looks like they may be gone, whoever they were." Taking a breath to brace herself, she stepped inside the front door. As she flipped on the lights, her breath rushed out of her, and despair quickly filled its place.

"Oh my God!"

Chapter Five

On Tuesday morning Chase stepped up onto the porch of the cabin marked "office" and knocked on the front door. When several moments passed with no response, he knocked again, louder this time. Lord, he was feeling irritable. He'd sat outside of Lacy's apartment building until midnight. When it became obvious she was in for the night, he finally gave up and went home. There was no point in getting over-tired, especially when he was starting a new job in the morning. A new job that meant no more early morning visits to the diner. But it was a small town. He was bound to run into her again, sooner or later. And next time, he'd get the job done.

He knocked one more time, then jammed his hands in his pockets and waited, not at all sure what to expect. One thing was for certain, the last thing he expected was to be greeted by a kid with dark, tousled hair wearing pajama pants.

"I'm looking for Shane," he told the kid.

"You must be Chase."

"That's right."

"I'm Mick. Come on in."

He followed Mick into the small office area where he'd been interviewed the day before. The boy led him through another door and into a tidy kitchen. "My dad had to go somewhere this morning. He said I should show you around. Mind if I take a quick shower first?"

Chase's nerves were jumping. The last thing he wanted was to sit around and wait, but how could he say that?

"Take your time."

"There's coffee in the coffee maker if you want it. It's Emma's girly stuff. I hope that's okay."

When Mick left the room, Chase walked over to inspect the coffee. Lifting the lid, he took a sniff. Vanilla. He sniffed again. Vanilla and some other spice he couldn't name. Shrugging, he poured himself a cup and carried it to the table. Girlie or not, he'd need all of the caffeine he could get to make it through this day. He'd wasted most of the night lying sleepless in his bed, tormented by thoughts of the lovely lady who slept in her own bed, just five blocks away.

A newspaper lay on the table, open to the sports section. He flipped through its pages until he found the Hope Haven police log. A forty-three-year-old man had been arrested for disorderly conduct. A south side woman was taken in on charges of aggravated assault. Nothing earth shaking there. At the top of the next page, a headline caught his eye: Burglary on Sandpiper Drive Makes Sixth in Area!

Chase read with interest about the break-in that had occurred the night before, the sixth in as many weeks. The owners, a Mr. and Mrs. Jeremy Holmes, had reportedly gone out to a meeting of the Sialia Society and returned home several hours later to find that their house had been ransacked. Although a number of priceless antiques had remained untouched, the couple reported the theft of a forty-two-inch flat screen television, some jewelry, and a small amount of cash. Mr. Holmes, a math teacher at Hope Haven High School, was reportedly grateful that the family heirlooms had not been stolen. Chase chewed his lip in thought. This was definitely not the work of a professional. A pro would have known the value of the antiques, but these perps had taken only cash, or items that could quickly be turned into cash.

He folded the paper and set it aside. There was only one reason he could think of for the rash of break-ins, and it wasn't good. Drug activity was as common as the rain in American cities all across the board. It was only a matter of time until it seeped down into the small towns. People were people, with the same weaknesses and greed, no matter where they lived. He knew that. Still, it made him angry. He'd always thought of Shadow Lake as the one uncorrupted place left in the world.

Despite himself, he started laying out the facts in his mind, turning them over one by one, like he'd turned over the pieces of his game of Concentration as a child. It wasn't his problem, or his job to figure it out. But the simple truth was he didn't know how not to think like a cop.

After several moments Mick reappeared, his hair towel dried, wearing a pair of jeans and a gray hoodie. "Sorry to make you wait, dude."

"No problem."

"I was planning to sleep in, since there's no school today. But then my dad got a phone call and him and Emma had to leave."

Chase studied the boy. "Where did you say he went?"

"He didn't say. Just told me he and Emma had to go out for a while, and I was supposed to show you around. Did he tell you about the carnival?"

"Yes, he mentioned it."

"Emma wants the whole campground decorated in icicle lights. So our job for today is to figure out how many we've gotta buy. Then later we'll have to start stringing them in the trees."

Mick's expression of dismay was comical and Chase smiled. "Well then, let's get crack-alacking, shall we?"

Mick's first order of business was to give Chase a tour of the campground, showing him the rec hall, the store, and the camp sites.

"There's another whole section of sites for the permanents, but all you really need to know about for now is the area, where Miss Emma's having her winter carnival." He led him to a clearing in the woods and pointed out a gazebo. "This is going to be Santa's Palace. Emma wants it decorated in big red bows and white lights. All of these trees will be done in blue icicles."

"All of them?"

"Yep. Miss Emma doesn't do things half way."

Chase whistled softly, calculating. "That's going to cost a fortune."

Mick grinned. "She says she doesn't care how much it costs." He pointed to a basketball court. "After we get the lights strung we have to box that in and flood it. Emma wants an ice skating rink for the kids."

Mick indicated the winding pathway. "She wants the trail lit, too. We're going to hire a farmer to give sleigh rides. Up near the rec hall there will be food booths and games. And she's holding a gingerbread house decorating contest, so we'll have to bring in buffet tables. She's also hiring a band, so we need to set up a platform. She says if she thinks of more things, she'll let us know."

"This sounds like quite an undertaking."

"It is. We had a stellar season and Emma wants to put on the carnival as a way of giving back to the community. Some of the money we make will be going to the food pantry. Miss Emma, she's good stuff."

Chase had met Emma Lucy briefly the day before. She was a lovely woman, and Shane Lucy was a lucky man. He felt a familiar aching in his gut. He'd always dreamed of finding a woman like that, someone to start a family with. But the life he'd chosen wasn't a good fit for a family man. It was filled with stress, late nights, and danger. But maybe it wasn't too late. Maybe now that things had changed he'd be able to find that someone and commit to a relationship. Thoughts of Lacy Kennedy flitted through his mind and he firmly pushed them away, reminding himself the arrangement was temporary. In three months he'd be returning to Queens. He'd pick up right where he left off, no worse for the wear.

The sound of heavy metal music sliced through the morning air, and Mick fished his cell phone out of his pocket. "Yo."

Chase watched the boy's face cloud over as he listened.

"She what? How do you know? Is he sure it was her?" He cursed under his breath. "Okay. Thanks."

He jammed his phone back in his pocket, his mood suddenly as gray as the November skies.

"Everything okay?" Chase asked.

"Not really." He was quiet for a moment, obviously trying to get himself under control. "Let's try to figure out how many strings of lights we need. I've got a feeling it's gonna be a long-ass day."

•

Polly took a moment to compose herself before opening her front door. "Shane, Emma, thank you so much for coming. I hated to bother you both, but I just didn't know who else to call."

"It's no problem, Polly," Shane said. "What's going on?"

She stepped aside to let him pass. Across the threshold, he stopped short, taking in the damage. "Holy cow."

"Oh, P-Polly." Emma wailed, her stutter betraying her dismay.

"Your beautiful c-cabinet."

Polly's antique china cabinet lay on its front, surrounded by shards of glass. Its doors were a twisted ruin. Once again, Shane's glance swept across the debris. "When did this happen?"

"I'm not sure, exactly. I went to my Sialia Society meeting last night. Afterward I had coffee with a friend. I got home a little after ten and found all of this." She lifted her hands in a gesture of helplessness. "Obviously someone broke in."

"What's missing? Have you made a list?"

She pressed a hand to her forehead, trying to think. Wendy's music thumped upstairs, setting her nerves on edge. When she'd mustered a small measure of composure, she said, "My television set, for one thing. And some jewelry. All of my good silver and my crystal goblets. And several bottles of wine and brandy are missing from the cellar." Thump. Thump. "It's a pity they didn't take that blasted CD player of hers."

"Thank God nobody was h-home." Emma slid her arms around Polly's shoulders. "Th-things can be replaced. People c-can't."

"Have you called the police?" Shane asked.

Polly's gaze dropped to the floor. "No, Shane, I haven't. And I'm not going to."

"But why, P-Polly? You need to report this."

"I can't, Emma." Polly struggled for a moment with her pride. She'd never been one to display her dirty linens in public. "The truth is, I just don't know what to think. You see, Wendy was home."

"She was here?" Shane asked, incredulous. "During the break-in?"

"So she says. She didn't go with me to the meeting because she said she didn't feel well. I phoned her around nine, and she said she was sleeping."

"So the break-in must have happened between nine and ten?"

"I called her on her cellular phone, Shane. She could have been anywhere. I certainly can't imagine anyone sleeping through the ruckus the thief must have made breaking through the door. Not to mention knocking over my china cabinet. I'm sure the girl's lying. I think she snuck out somewhere and arrived home shortly before I did, but she won't admit it. So you see, I can't alert the police. They'll ask questions. Questions neither Wendy nor I can truthfully answer."

"Even so," Shane said. "There was another break-in on the lake last night, over on Sandpiper Drive. If the police knew there were two break-ins it might make a difference. Maybe somebody saw something that would help them catch the guy."

"I'm sorry, Shane. I just can't. I can easily replace the television. And the jewelry was just old costume pieces. I never wore them anyway. I'd rather count my losses than have Wendy scrutinized by the police."

Shane looked as though he was about to protest again, but Emma laid a hand on his arm. "What can we do to help you, Polly?"

"If you could repair the door, and maybe replace the locks, I'd feel so much safer."

Shane examined the door. "I've got my tool box out in the truck. I'll repair these hinges and then go to the hardware store for new locks, both front and back."

"Bless you."

As soon as he left the house, Emma began to sort through the debris. She scooped up the dirt from an upended spider plant and placed it back in its pot. "P-poor baby. Here, I'll fix you up good as new."

"Don't fuss, Emma. I can clean this up."

"I don't mind. Believe it or n-not, the same thing happen to me last year. I can't imagine how I would have m-managed if Shane hadn't helped me out."

Polly had heard the story many times of how Emma's apartment in a downtown alley had been vandalized, how Shane had come to her rescue like a white knight, given her shelter at the campground, and eventually, married her. It was the lake community's very own fairy tale. But right now she had less fanciful things to think about.

"Actually, Emma, there's something else I'd rather have you do."

Emma stood. "Anything."

"Would you go upstairs and talk to Wendy? I can't seem to get the truth out of her."

"What would you like me to say?"

Polly sighed. "I don't know where she was last night ... if you could just caution her about sneaking around ... about boys." She felt her face grow warm. "I've tried, but she thinks of me as an ancient old fool."

"I'll do my b-best, Polly."

Polly watched as Emma disappeared up the staircase. Within moments the racket of Wendy's music was silenced and Polly let out her breath, thanking God for small favors.

Chapter Six

Lacy was having a tough time keeping her mind on her work. Her head ached and her stomach churned with worry. She was barely three hours into her shift, and already she'd delivered three meals to the wrong tables, forgotten to refill four water glasses, and just now she'd served Zechariah Bowman decaffeinated coffee instead of regular. He was the nicest man in town—until it came to his coffee. She was acing like a total scatterbrain. She sighed. On top of everything else, it would be a skimpy day for tips.

A dense fog seemed to have settled over her, one she couldn't find her way out of. Despite a heroic effort to keep her mind on task, her thoughts kept sliding back to the previous night. As if it wasn't bad enough that she'd had a cop sitting in front of her apartment building all night, staking her out as if she were some sort of criminal, when she'd finally managed to fall asleep, she'd dreamed about Angel.

In her dream, they laughed as they ran toward a carousel. She recognized the park from a summer vacation she'd taken to Ohio with the Kruger's many years before. It had been a lovely day, her first time ever at an amusement park, and she'd been mesmerized by the plethora of new experiences. She'd loved the thrill of riding on the spinning tops and the excitement of the arcades. She'd loved the fun house and the pale blue cotton candy. But most of all, she'd loved the painted ponies on the carousel.

The dream brought it back to her with startling clarity—the sights, sounds and smells of that long-ago day. At the dream's onset, she felt all of the familiar excitement, but as she and Angel drew closer to the carousel, the scenery changed. The cobbled walkways became littered with weeds, and she and Angel picked their way through them in search of the golden pony. The sky above threatened rain as they hurried past the abandoned fun house, its windows smashed and its once cheerful paint faded and blistering. When they reached the carousel, Angel climbed onto their pony; pale gold with a cream-colored mane. Smiling, he held out his hands to her and lifted her on behind him. The music began. There was no attendant, but as if by pure magic, the ponies started to revolve.

The sky grew darker as she rode 'round and 'round, her arms wrapped tightly around Angel's waist. Then, suddenly, the golden pony was a real stallion, and they galloped, breathless, across an open field under a moonlit sky. As the horse sped onward, her initial feelings of freedom and exhilaration were swallowed up by fear. Angel shouted something she couldn't hear, his words whipped away on the wind. And then he vanished and she was alone on the stallion, racing out of control.

The dream left her shaken and filled with a strange foreboding.

"Hey, Beautiful."

The words were low, but close. Startled, she turned to see Brandon Blake leaning across the counter.

"Oh. Hi, Brandon."

"Hey, we're playing at the Knuckleheads on Friday night. Gonna be a hell of a party afterwards. Wanna come?"

"Sorry. I've got plans."

"Aww, come on. What could be more important?"

"I have to go to the Laundromat."

The comment drew laughs from Brandon's buddies.

"You know, Lace, I really get tired of this love-hate relationship of ours."

She grabbed the carafe from beneath the coffee maker. "You and I don't have a relationship, Brandon, love-hate or any other kind. Excuse me," brushing past him, she carried the coffee pot to Mr. Bowman's table. When she returned to the counter, Brandon was still there, fiddling with a napkin holder. "So when are you gonna go out with me?"

"Look, Brandon, I'm busy. All I'm going to say about that is don't hold your breath, okay?"

She breezed past him and disappeared into the kitchen, in no mood today for his nonsense. Brandon was as cute as they came, but he was a starving singer in a two-bit garage band. His life was going absolutely nowhere, and she wasn't about to go there with him. She wouldn't make that mistake. Not again.

Stop it, Lacy! she scolded herself. Stop thinking about Angel.

But she couldn't seem to help herself. She pondered the feelings of tenderness the dream evoked, and the uneasiness. She'd been having the exact same dream for about three weeks now. Not every night, but often enough that it troubled her.

She sighed. Like it or not, she and Angel had a connection. When they were lovers she knew instinctively when he was in trouble. Just as she knew now, on some visceral level, that something bad had happened to him. And while she didn't want him in her life, Lord ... she hated to think of him no longer in the world.

Unnerved, she walked to the bathroom and splashed a handful of cold water on her face. Patting it dry with a paper towel, she gazed at the hard lessons time had etched into her face. It wouldn't have had to be this way, she thought. This isn't the way I wanted it to end for us.

Memories surfaced, like dark angels in her mind and she was powerless to stave them off. She thought back to when she and Angel first met, back to when times were good.

After the Krugers moved away, Lacy crawled back into her world of isolation. Her new stepfather made it clear their small apartment wasn't big enough for both of them, so Lacy started hanging out on the streets, desperate to find a place where she belonged. She started experimenting with alcohol and marijuana. Anything to ease the pain of being unwanted.

High school was a lonely, miserable place for Lacy, so she dropped out the day she turned sixteen and got a part-time job at the video store on Merchant Street. Lacy thought it was a good deal. She got a paycheck each week, and besides that, she got to watch all of the latest movies for free. The down side of it was that she was often scheduled to work until the store closed at midnight, which meant walking home through the worst section of town late at night. She bought a can of pepper spray with her first paycheck.

One balmy Friday night a Latino boy a few years older than she pulled up beside her in a rattletrap car. "Where are you going, Chica?"

She quickened her pace, ignoring him.

Undeterred, he drove along beside her as she walked. "Hey, you need a ride somewhere?"

She slipped her hand in her pocket, closing it around the vial of pepper spray.

"Pretty little girl like you shouldn't be out here at night. It ain't safe."

"Get lost."

To her dismay, he followed her all the way home. A half block past her mother's building, she ducked into the doorway of another apartment house, holding her breath until he gunned the engine and drove away.

The following night he was there again. Lacy took the same route, ducking into the doorway of the same apartment building and doubling back home after he'd gone. On the third night, he rolled down the window and talked to her while she walked, making jokes about being her guardian angel. On the fourth night, she left work to find the skies pouring rain. On that night, she finally allowed him to give her a ride home. On that night, she fell in love with his cocoa-brown eyes and his lazy smile. He won her over one smile at a time, masquerading as the savior she was so badly in need of.

After that, he took her to the movies most every Saturday afternoon. His friend, Mario, who worked at the local theater, would smuggle them in the back door when no one was watching. On Sundays they drove to a secluded spot on the lake and talked for hours. Angel told her he'd been in the foster care system since he was twelve, and his brother, Tito, was five. He'd grown up eating table scraps, while his foster parents' real children ate like kings, or so he said. He got a job at the local Shop-N-Save when he was eighteen and started saving his paychecks, vowing to one day become a millionaire. He promised Lacy that when he made his first million he'd marry her, and they'd never be poor again.

A few months after they started dating, Angel began taking her to fancy restaurants. He moved out of his rented room at the YMCA and into a medium-sized brick house on Bolton Street. When Lacy asked him how he was able to afford a down payment on a minimum wage job a grocery store, he smiled. "Hard work, Chica. That's all you gotta know."

If it occurred to her that he had more money than he should have, she didn't question it.

After a few months he asked her to move in with him, and Lacy packed her belongings into a cardboard box and left her mother's house without a backward glance. No one ever came looking for her, and sometimes Lacy wondered if her mother had even noticed she was gone.

"Take your break, Kiddo."

Doreen's voice scattered her thoughts and she glanced at her watch. Two o'clock. Two more hours to go. God, she was tired.

•

"I just don't need all the frickin' drama, ya know?"

Oh, hell, Chase thought. *So we're back to that, are we?*

The snippet of that morning's phone conversation he'd overheard told Chase the boy's troubles were of the female variety. It was certainly none of his business, and hell, he didn't care either way. But he had to talk to the kid about something, didn't he? And getting people to talk was something Chase was good at. Working undercover for three years, he'd learned the secret to getting people to open up, even when they didn't want to. Basically, it came down to showing an interest. Get people talking about themselves, he'd learned, and ninety-nine times out of one hundred, they'd tell you their life stories. Which was what Mick was doing now.

"Get used to it, pal," he said. "You want a woman, you're gonna get drama. It's a package deal. Are there any more lights left?"

They'd bought six hundred and twenty-five feet of lights, and by noon they'd strung them in sixty-seven trees. And still the path was only half lit. Chase rubbed his aching muscles. It had been awhile since he'd put in a hard day's physical labor. He'd been out of work for three weeks. Away from the gym for twice that long. He was starting to atrophy. Get soft. Not good.

"We already used up all the lights we bought. Man, did you screw up or what?"

"I have lot of strengths, but being a mathematical genius isn't one of them. And besides, you screwed up right along with me."

Mick grinned for the first time since he'd gotten the phone call that morning. "We'll have to go back into town and get more lights. But first let's have lunch. I'm starving."

Back at the house, they piled their plates with ham sandwiches and potato chips. Chase dug in, ravenous.

"I mean, Wendy's cute, and she's fun to be with," Mick said. "But she's not the person I thought she was. Know what I mean?"

"I do know what you mean."

"It was all good when she was hanging out with me, but then she started hanging with the wrong crowd."

"It happens." Chase took another bite of his sandwich, Mick's words resonating deeply.

"I mean, her aunt, Polly Church? She took Wendy in when her mother went to jail. And Wendy repaid her by stealing her booze and giving it to her low-life friends for their parties."

Chase turned that piece of the puzzle over in his mind and then filed it away. "People have a lot of reasons for doing what they do, Mick."

"If she's got a reason for hanging out in a bad part of town late at night, I don't think I want to know what it is." He was quiet for a long moment. "The thing is, I don't think I'm ready to give up on her."

Chase finished the last bite of his sandwich and washed it down with a bottle of water. "Then don't."

Driving home that afternoon, Chase was still thinking about the conversation. Images of Angel swirled in his memory, haunting him. I'm not ready to give up on her, Mick had said. Chase knew all about that, about giving up too soon.

Mick said Wendy had started hanging with the wrong crowd. Hanging in a bad section of town. He wondered what had brought about the sudden change in the girl. He thought about what Mick had said about Wendy stealing her aunt's booze and wondered if there was any connection to her and the recent break-ins around the lake. His cell phone rang, sending the puzzle pieces spinning from his mind.

"Yeah."

"Hello, Chase?"

"Hey. What's up, Maxie?"

"How did it go today, hon?"

"All right."

"I'm glad. Hey, would it be too much trouble to ask you to stop by the store on your way home and pick up a gallon of milk and some whipped cream? I'm making gingerbread."

He groaned. "Max, I'm going to gain a hundred pounds if you keep this up."

"Well, just what are the holidays for, if a mother can't spoil her favorite boy?" she scolded.

He smiled. "All right, Max, keep the gingerbread warm. I'll be home in about fifteen minutes."

He took a left onto Arbor Street and pulled to the curb in front of Castillo's Market. Inside, he strode to the cooler and retrieved a carton of milk and a container of whipped topping. Back up front, he set the items on the counter and grabbed a newspaper from the rack. The door opened, sending a blast of cold air sweeping over him. He looked up from his paper to see Lacy Kennedy standing in the doorway. Her glance swept over him in surprise. Before he could react, she turned and walked out.

"I'll be right back, sweetheart," he told the startled cashier. Tossing his paper on the counter, he hurried after her. She was already a half a block away, and moving quickly.

"Lacy!" he called.

She kept walking, quickening her pace. Moments later, she turned a corner and was gone. He could have easily caught up with her, but thought better of it. The timing didn't seem right, and this definitely wasn't the place. Back inside, he paid for his items. Slinging the bag over his shoulder, he walked back outside. Lacy leaned against his car, her expression colder than the winter air.

"What do you want from me?" she demanded.

A hundred words filled his brain, but now was not the time to say them. But he was the one who'd called her out. He had to say something, and so he blurted, "I have news for you. About Angel."

She flinched, then quickly recovered. "I don't want to hear it."

"Okay."

"Angel De la Fuente is nothing to me any more. He hasn't been for a long, long time. So whatever he sent you here to tell me, you can shove—"

"Lacy." He blew out a breath. "Angel's dead."

The color drained from her face. "What?" she whispered.

"I'm sorry, Lacy. He's gone. I've been trying to find a way to tell you."

Tears sprang to her eyes and she furiously wiped them away. "Like I said, it's nothing to me. So just leave me alone, got it?" She turned and hurried across the street, turned the corner at Wysteria Avenue, and disappeared.

Chapter Seven

The average life span of a female bluebird is six point seven years. The average human female's life expectancy is eighty point four. But of course, even the law of averages has its exceptions. On Friday evening Polly sat at the dining room table, pushing her food around on her plate and doing her best to ignore the sullen girl who sat across from her. Lord. At times like these she felt one hundred and sixty point eight.

The past few days had taken a toll on her—the break-in, Wendy's blatant disobedience. And as if that weren't enough to deal with, she had an appointment with Doctor Logan in the morning. She didn't know if she had the strength. Just thinking about it, the few bites of roast beef she'd swallowed threatened to come up. Tomorrow her fears would either be allayed or confirmed.

She glanced at her niece, who showed no more interest in the roast than she. She would have given anything to avoid the confrontation that was bound to erupt, but with no way around it, she cleared her throat and plunged in.

"I spoke with Emma Lucy today."

Wendy looked up from her plate and Polly forced a smile. "It seems she needs some help tomorrow baking cookies for her winter carnival. I volunteered your services."

Wendy's expression betrayed her annoyance. "All right. But you're the Betty Crocker around here. Shouldn't you be the one going?"

"Actually, yes, I suppose I should. But I have an appointment in the city tomorrow morning."

She waited for the words to sink in and saw her niece's face change from apathy to anger once they had. "You've got to be kidding me."

She sighed. "Wendy—"

"I'm grounded, Aunt Polly. I get that. You don't need to have Mrs. Lucy baby-sit me just because you're going out for the day."

"It doesn't have a thing to do with babysitting."

"Bull shit."

"Watch your mouth, young lady!"

"I'm not a child, Aunt Polly. I can stay by myself."

"I just thought it would be better this way."

"Why?"

"Well, considering Monday night's events …"

"So I made a mistake. So what? That means you can't ever trust me again?"

"I'm only trying to avoid trouble."

"I'm not going to get in any trouble!"

"I guess you'll have to prove that to me." She gave the girl a level stare. "I shudder to think what would have happened if I'd called the police that night. The questions they would have asked …"

Wendy jumped to her feet, sending her chair toppling backward. "Why don't you call them, then? Call them right now and tell them I snuck out without permission. Tell them I'm guilty of wanting to actually have a life! Maybe they'll haul me off to jail. Maybe they'll lock me up and throw away the frickin' key. Wouldn't that be a break!"

She stormed from the room, pounded up the stairs, and slammed her bedroom door. Moments later her music came on at an ear shattering volume.

Polly pushed her plate away. Despite her resolve to be strong, her eyes filled with tears. Rather than brush them away, she let them fall, acknowledging them as part of an inner healing. She closed her eyes, letting this new sorrow blend with old sorrows, knowing that to embrace her life experiences, both good and bad, would heal her, in the end.

When she opened the floodgates that normally held back her sorrows, the memory of the baby bluebirds was always the first to come. Nearly thirty years had passed, but still, the day of the bluebirds ached like a fresh wound in Polly's heart. Her tears fell harder as she saw herself retrieving their broken bodies from the dirt, saw Benny's cruel smirk as she tried in vain to save them. Her husband was a mean-spirited man, and all these years after his death she was still not free of the pain his life had brought her.

He'd ridiculed her obsession with the bluebirds that colored the trees outside her window, had belittled the lopsided nest box she'd built from scraps of wood and placed in a thicket. But even Benny's derision could not overshadow the hours of joy the birds brought her as she stood, binoculars in hand, watching the male and female bluebirds build their nest. Oh, the joy and pride she felt when the four beautiful, turquoise-blue eggs became four tiny babies.

One misty June morning, she glanced out her window and saw frenzied activity as the male and female bluebirds relentlessly circled the nest box. Knowing something must be terribly wrong, she pulled on her house coat and hurried outside. Heart pounding, she raced across the yard, where the gray face of a house sparrow peeked from the hole of the nest box.

"Oh no," she whispered. "Please, Lord. No."

The house sparrow darted away as she drew nearer, but the damage had already been done. With tears blurring her vision, she knelt to retrieve the broken bodies of the baby bluebirds from the dirt. Cradling them in her hands, she'd traced her thumb across the soft fuzz of their unformed feathers, across the vicious holes in their tiny bodies caused by the sparrow's crushing beak.

Discovering two of the babies still alive, she'd taken them inside and placed them in soft bed of cotton. She'd hovered over them, kept them warm, fed them bits of bread soaked in milk. They'd died the next morning.

"That's what happens when humans go messin' with nature, gal," Benny had chided. "What did you expect?"

A miracle, her heart cried. I expected a miracle! Somehow, she'd believed her love could save them.

Rather than discourage her, Benny's words only made her more determined than ever. That afternoon, she went to the library and checked out a stack of books on song birds. She read and she read, soaking up the information like a dry and thirsty sponge. In the years since, she'd rehabbed more birds than she could count; blue jays and robins who'd suffered unfortunate encounters with untended cats, a screech owl with a broken wing, and dozens of chickadees, phoebes and wrens who'd crashed against her neighbor's windows.

Wendy's music stopped abruptly. Wiping her eyes on the sleeve of her sweater, Polly stood and began to clear the table. She only wished she knew how to rehab a young girl with a broken heart.

•

"You're quiet tonight," Maxine commented.

Chase drew his attention away from his dinner plate to meet his foster mother's eyes. Her expression was one he knew well - anxious, concerned, kind. He smiled. "I'm fine, Max. Just tired."

"So tell me. How did your first week go?"

"Busy. But good."

"What have they got you doing?" She leaned toward him, her expression one of pure curiosity. He'd been close mouthed about his new job all week, but one look at her face told him he'd not get away with evasiveness this evening.

"Well, let's see. On Tuesday and Wednesday we strung enough lights to decorate a small forest. All blue and white."

"I'll bet it's breathtaking."

"It is. On Thursday we built a skating rink, and today we transformed a gazebo into Santa's palace." He swallowed a forkful of chicken and dumplings. "Next week, who knows?"

"It sounds like an awful lot of work. Shane's lucky to have you."

"I'm lucky to have the job. It keeps my mind occupied."

She hesitated. "Are you going to be staying for awhile, Chase?"

"For awhile. If you can put up with me while I get my head together."

"That's my pleasure and my privilege, Child."

She gave him another inquiring glance, but didn't ask any more questions. He was grateful to her for not prying into his personal business. He wasn't ready yet, to tell his story. To admit how badly he'd screwed up. Not even to this woman who'd raised him like her own son.

Sensing his discomfort, Maxine changed the subject. "What do you make of these awful robberies?

"Drug related, probably."

Her glance was startled. "Why do you say that?"

"When people start feeling desperate enough for money that they'll rob houses, it's usually because of drugs."

"Mercy. I hate to think that Shadow Lake's coming to that."

"Me too, Max. But six robberies in six weeks. I don't know what else to think."

"There have been seven, actually. My friend, Polly Church, had her house broken into the other night."

He glanced up. "Same neighborhood as the others?"

"Same side of the lake. She lives on October Lane, over in Sackett's Harbor."

"I don't remember hearing about that one."

"That's because she didn't report the burglary to the authorities."

"Why not?"

"She was vague about her reasons. Said nothing much had been taken. Some old costume jewelry, a television she was going to replace anyway. Oh, and a few bottles of her homemade wine."

As Chase digested the information, two of the puzzle pieces clicked into place. "Be that as it may, she still should have reported it to the police."

"She doesn't want anyone to know and I probably shouldn't have mentioned it." She stood and began to clear the serving dishes from the table.

"Your secrets are safe with me, Maxie." He retrieved his plate and silverware and followed her to the kitchen, where she busily filled the sink with water. "Do you want help with these?" he asked.

"No, dear. But thanks for offering."

"Thanks for dinner. It was delicious." He planted a kiss on her cheek. "I'm going to go out for a little while."

"All right, dear. Drive carefully."

Thirty minutes later, he was cruising through Polly Church's neighborhood. Sackett's Harbor was one of the nicest areas in the lake community. Polly's home was not as grand as some of the other houses that had been burglarized, but the fact that it was shrouded in trees made it a prime target. Easy access. The perpetrator was likely in and out within minutes, with no one the wiser. He drummed his fingertips on the steering wheel. Why hadn't the old woman told the police? He thought about what Mick had said about his girlfriend stealing her aunt's booze. Unless he missed his guess, the old woman was protecting her.

He spent the next forty minutes checking out the other houses that had been broken into. Some of them were large and oozing with wealth, and some were more modest, like Polly Church's. He studied each of them in turn, looking for a common link.

An hour later he was back in Sunset Cove. Experience told him that bars were the best source of information. Especially small, seedy places like The Brass Bull. And especially on Friday evenings, when alcohol softened the blow of a long, hard work week and loosened tongues.

Parking his car in the lot, he pulled up the collar of his jacket and made a bee line across the street. The air inside the bar was close and dank, but even so, it provided a welcome respite from the cold. He sat down at the bar and ordered a beer, shooting glances in the mirror, taking in the scenery. Barely eight o'clock, and already the place was crowded. He'd come five or six times before and the locals were getting used to him. He let himself relax, absorbing the driving beat of the music and the dull roar of conversation. He kept his eyes on the sports program on the television above the bar, his ears trained on the conversation around him.

A man of about his age approached the table behind him and a leathery-faced older man, already well on his way to oblivion, hollered out a greeting. "Hey, Jimmy, I been tryin' to get ahold of you. We playing poker on Wednesday night, or what?"

"Can't do it, man. I got double shifts all next week."

"Aw, hell. That kind of schedule will put ya in your grave, son."

"Don't I know it. But I got a balloon payment due on my old lady's car at the end of the month. She loses that car, she'll divorce me."

Laughter blended with the music. There was talk about the local canning factory. About wives and co-workers and kids. Braces and car payments and mortgages. He listened, sorting through the words, picking out the names. Marcus White. Johnny Boo. Big Larry. Jackie Smack. Behind him, a fragment of conversation caught his interest.

"Hey, you seen Johnny Dog's new truck yet?"

"Johnny Dog ain't got no new truck."

"The hell he don't. Just got it today. Said the dealership delivered the son-of-a-gun with a full tank of gas."

"Dang. How'd he do it?"

"Won thirty freakin' grand on a four-way lottery split. I'd love to have that guy's freakin' luck."

It was the sort of information that could be useful, and Chase filed it away, making a mental note to keep his ears open for more information about Johnny Dog and his winning lottery ticket. He swallowed the last of his beer and was signaling for another when a figure out on the sidewalk caught his eye -- a raven-haired woman in a fawn-colored jacket. He took note of the laundry basket in her hands, of the cold, hate-filled eyes staring into his, and he began to sweat. His last conversation with her had been weighing heavily on him. He'd meant to break the news to her gently, and instead he'd hurled it at her with all the finesse of a tsunami. For as long as he lived, he wouldn't forgive himself for the pain he'd put in her eyes. He'd begged the powers that be for another chance, a chance to make it right. And now the chance had landed square in his lap, and he wasn't even close to prepared for it. Even so, he threw a five-dollar bill on the bar and went outside to meet her.

•

When Lacy had told Brandon she planned to spend Friday night doing laundry, she was lying. At the time, the last thing on her mind was a trip to the Laundromat. But after three evenings of sitting around her apartment, crying, she felt the need to get out and do something. And since she was down to her last clean uniform, doing laundry seemed as good a plan as any.

Folding the last of her freshly dried clothes, she packed them into her laundry basket, zipped up her coat, and headed out into the night. Damn, it was cold. She couldn't remember a colder December.

Quickening her pace, she shot glances into the windows of the buildings as she passed. Most of them were abandoned, except for a handful of bars and a liquor store. Not the greatest area to be walking in alone at night, but at least it was still fairly early. And she'd never given up the habit of carrying a can of pepper spray in her purse. Passing by the Brass Bull, she glanced into the window, stopping short when she saw the blond stranger sitting at the bar.

She stared at him in disbelief, her heart pounding with rage. Seconds later, his eyes met hers. She would have liked to shake her fist at him, but her hands were occupied with the laundry basket. Now that he'd seen her, she wanted to run away, but all she could do was stand there, glaring at him through the window. She watched as he pulled a bill from his pocket and threw it down on the bar. Moments later, the door opened and he appeared on the sidewalk.

"Evening, Lacy."

"You're unbelievable, you know that? Why are you stalking me?"

"I'm not stalking you. I'm having a beer."

"Why here? In my neighborhood?"

"It's my neighborhood, too. I grew up here."

Disbelief colored her angry eyes. "I know everyone around here, and I've never seen you until a few days ago."

"I've been gone awhile. Now I'm back."

"I don't know what your game is, but I want you to stay away from me, understand?"

"I don't have a game. And I'm not trying to cause any trouble. I just wanted to say I'm sorry."

"For what?"

"For the other day. I shouldn't have blurted it out like that."

"I told you, I don't care."

"The look on your face made me think you do."

She paused, her resolve wavering. She'd gotten good at hiding her feelings. Obviously he was better at reading them. Because she did care. More than she wanted to admit.

"How did he die?" she finally asked.

"He was shot."

She closed her eyes against the wave of pain that rippled through her. "Who shot him?"

"I did."

Despite her resolve, a sob escaped her. She brushed past him, walking briskly.

"Lacy, wait." He laid a hand on her arm and she flinched.

"Don't touch me. Don't you ever touch me."

"I'm sorry." His hand fell back to his side. "Look, there are things I want to tell you. Things Angel wanted you to know. Can we go somewhere and talk? Somewhere warm?"

His nerve was astounding. Did he really think she'd talk to him now, after he'd confessed to being Angel's killer? "I don't have time."

"Just have a cup of coffee with me. One cup of coffee. Twenty minutes. And then I promise I'll leave you alone."

A part of her wanted to keep walking, far away from him, to the ends of the earth where she'd never have to see him again. But the bigger part was anxious to hear what he had to say. "I've got to take my laundry home. I'll meet you at Sherry's Diner in ten minutes."

After walking the last few blocks home, she rushed up the stairs and dumped the laundry basket on her bed. Glancing at the clock, she saw that ten minutes had already passed. For a moment she considered not going. But Lacy wasn't the type of woman to run away from the truth. Even when it hurt like hell. She needed closure, and this man was the only one who could give it to her.

Fifteen minutes later, she walked into the diner and saw him sitting in a booth near the back. She took a breath to fortify herself, and then she took a step forward. Two cups of coffee steamed on the table in front of him.

"I ordered our coffee," he said.

She slid into the booth across from him, pulled off her hat, and shook out her hair.

"You've got twenty minutes. Start talking."

Chapter Eight

Chase had been deep undercover for nine months when Angel De la Fuente was released from prison. Angel had been nabbed upstate for drug trafficking and sentenced to Rikers Island in New York City for six to ten years. He was back on the streets in three and a half.

Angel started his life as a free man with the best of intentions. He thought that if he could make an honest living, if he could prove to himself that he could walk the straight and narrow, he could go back home. Back to Lacy. He got a job delivering furniture forty hours a week. It was backbreaking work for which he received very little pay and even less respect. He lasted two weeks.

Unable to resist the temptation of easy money, he looked up his old cell mate, Johnny Red. On Johnny's recommendation, gang leader Soy Spade accepted Angel into The Diamondbacks, one of the toughest street gangs in Queens. That's when he first met Chase Alexander, known to The Diamonds as White Snake. They were both in over their heads, but neither knew it until it was too late.

Angel stepped back into his life of crime as easily as a badger steps into a trap. After his initiation, a brutal beating dispensed by each member of the gang, Johnny put Angel to work selling drugs on the street. Proving himself to be a good money-maker, Johnny promoted Angel to bigger crimes, and he started stealing cars and robbing houses, and Chase was appointed his mentor.

Their first week together, they were doing reconnaissance, cruising the neighborhood, looking for vulnerable residences, cars left unattended, when Angel lit up a pipe and passed it across to Chase.

"What the hell are you doing? We just passed a cop, you idiot."

"Ain't no cops gonna bother us."

"Get rid of that damned thing. Now."

Grumbling, Angel snuffed out the pipe and stowed it in his pocket. "So what are you supposed to be, man? Some kind of priest?"

Chase was ready with his standard answer. "Selling the product's one thing. Nobody ever made any money by using it. I thought you were smarter than that."

Angel studied him, long and hard. Finally he said, "Where you from, man?"

Chase's hands tensed on the wheel. "Nowhere."

"You remind me of this dude that used to go to my school."

Chase's heart constricted. There was no way he could possibly have any connection to Angel, but being made was an undercover cop's worst nightmare. "Yeah? Well I was never big on going to school."

Angel snorted. "Who the hell was?"

After a few long moments, Angel said, "I kind of wish I'd of finished, though."

Chase shrugged. "I'm doing okay without it."

"I am, too. But I had a girl back home. If I'd of flown straight instead of going to jail, if I could' a had a career, things might of worked out with her."

"There's lots of girls."

"Yeah. But not like her."

Chase pulled into a Burger Baron parking lot. "I'm gonna get a burger."

They went inside, ordered their food, and sat down at a table. Chase picked up his burger and took a bite.

"Me and Lacy, we were supposed to get married," Angel said. "I gave her a diamond ring two weeks before I got busted."

"If she was so damn great, why don't you get back with her?"

"I don't wanna mess her up. And besides, she won't have nothing to do with me now. And anyway, ain't no way in hell I can go back to Shadow Lake. Not yet."

The burger stuck in Chase's throat. He choked it down. "What the hell's Shadow Lake?"

"It's where I grew up."

"Sounds pretty fancy for a street punk."

Angel laughed. "It is. But every fancy place has its toilet, you know? Shadow Lake's is a place called Sunset Cove. That's where I grew up."

Chase forced himself to look Angel square in the eye. "Never heard of it."

Angel shrugged. "No reason you would."

He was cool as steel on the outside, but inside, Chase's nerves were screaming. This changed things. Made the whole thing risky. One mistake, one wrong word could cost him the investigation. Not to mention his life.

He'd think about it later, and think that if he could turn back time, back to that exact moment, he'd bail out and not look back. To hell with the nine months he'd invested, and the fact that he had almost enough evidence to blow a city-wide drug cartel wide open. Sitting in a booth with Angel De la Fuente in a filthy burger joint, his gut told him to abandon the project. For the first time ever, he ignored it.

In three years working undercover detail, the one thing Chase had learned was never to trust a drug addict. He'd been warned that developing sympathy for the criminal was one of the pitfalls of the job, but it had never happened to him personally. Not until he met Angel. Over the next few weeks he and Angel formed a strange friendship and he broke the cardinal rule. Beneath his street-hardened exterior, Angel had a quality of vulnerability about him, a masked, innate sort of goodness. He was a good man who'd made some bad mistakes, and despite himself, Chase genuinely liked him.

Belonging to a street gang isn't as sensational in reality as it is in the movies. A gang member spends most of his days sleeping, his nights stealing cars and selling drugs. Over the course of a few weeks, he and Angel stole a lot of cars. They drank a lot of booze. And they talked.

When he was sober, Angel was introspective and distant. When he drank, he became philosophical. He talked about his upbringing, and about his little brother, Tito. He talked about Lacy. He rationalized his drug activity, saying that as soon as he got enough money to give Tito and Lacy a good life, he'd get out.

Even under the influence, Chase was careful. He let Angel talk, all the while silently gathering information, culling the conversation for pieces he could use, disregarding the rest. Above all, he was careful. But give him enough time, even the most circumspect soldier gets sloppy. He gets overconfident, messes up, and Chase messed up royally. One humid summer night, after too much beer and too much talk, he carelessly mentioned a Hope Haven tavern.

Angel regarded him through slitted eyes. "How do you know that?"

Realizing his mistake immediately, Chase struggled for control, made his face impassive. "You told me, dude."

"I told you about Knuckleheads? When?"

"I don't know, man," he barked. "You must have. How the hell else would I know?"

Three days later he woke up to the unmistakable click of a safety catch being released. He opened his eyes and found himself staring into the barrel of a 38-caliber, snub-nose hand gun. At one time the weapons were standard-issue police guns. Now they could be had on the streets for a song.

He pulled in a silent breath. "What the hell you think you're doing?"

"I'm doing you a favor, man." Angel's voice was unnaturally high-pitched. Bone chillingly cold.

"How've you got that figured?"

"Wounds from a friend beat the hell out of kisses from an enemy, ain't that what the Bible says? The way I see it, either I shoot you clean, or I let Spade torture you to death."

"Why would he do that?"

"Because you're a cop." He spat the word. His tongue darted out to catch the beads of sweat forming on his upper lip. "I may be a dumb bastard, but I finally figured it out. I never felt right about you from the start. I didn't wanna believe it, man, because I liked you. But that kid that used to go to my school? That kid - he took all the cop classes." His voice cracked. "That kid was you."

Chase's senses were on red alert. His glance took in the entire scenario in an instant, calculating, considering his options. He outweighed Angel by at least forty pounds. He had a nine millimeter Glock under his pillow. He had the brains and the brawn to extract himself from the situation. All he needed was the opportunity.

"Lay it down, Angel. Let's talk about your options."

"No way." The gun trembled in his hand. "I ain't going back to prison for nobody."

"Maybe you won't have to. Just give me some information. I'll see what I can do."

"Shut up, man. I'm the one making the decisions here, so just shut the hell up!"

He was nervous, breaking down. Chase thought of the one thing that would break him completely. "What about Lacy? Kill a cop and you can kiss her goodbye."

Angel hesitated. Not much, but enough. Throwing his weight behind him, Chase rolled from the mattress and onto the floor, catching Angel around the ankles. The other man toppled forward. Chase grabbed the Glock from beneath his pillow, but not before the crash of Angel's handgun split the air. He missed Chase's head by a fraction of an inch. Before the man in Chase could back down, the cop in him pulled back the hammer and fired.

In the seconds between the thunder of gunfire and the driving rain of Chase's guilt, Angel fell back to his knees, and his disbelieving eyes locked on Chase's in a moment that time would never erase.

•

When he'd finished speaking, Chase sat, silent. Long moments passed. Finally, he said, "I'm sorry, Lacy. It wasn't the way I wanted it to end."

Lacy brushed a stream of tears from her face. "I knew, deep down. I knew he was gone. I had a dream. I just … I didn't want it to be true."

He gently brushed his thumb across her face, erasing the last of her tears. "I thought when it was all over, when the dust settled, I could help him get his life back together. I really wanted to do that."

"Angel was too addicted to money. He never would have walked a straight line. Not even for me." She pulled a napkin from the dispenser and daintily blew her nose. "So what made you come back to Sunset Cove?"

"I didn't know where else to go." He shrugged. "I guess I wanted to try and put closure on some things."

"By telling me about how it went down?"

"He never stopped loving you. I thought you should know, that's all."

"Why didn't he let me know he was out of prison? Why didn't he come home?"

"He thought you'd be better off without him. He wanted you to have a good life. I guess he knew you couldn't have that with him."

"Thank you," she said softly. "For telling me."

She was lovely, her hair wind-tossed and wild, her eyes wet with tears. He ached to draw her into his arms, to comfort her. To kiss her. But those kinds of thoughts wouldn't help anyone, so he pushed them from his mind.

"He was worried about his kid brother, afraid he might be getting into some bad stuff," he said.

"Tito?"

"You know him?"

"Sure, I know Tito. I haven't seen him around in awhile, though. What kind of bad stuff?"

"He didn't say, but I can guess. Does Tito have a job?"

"Last I knew he was working down on the docks. Why?"

"I just want to check on him, see if he's up to anything he shouldn't be."

She nodded.

"Would you be willing to help me get the lay of the land?" he asked. "Show me some of the places Tito hangs out?"

"I'm sorry for Tito, if he's messing up his life. But I don't want to go back there. Back to the places I used to hang out with Angel. It's not good for my head."

"Would you be willing to ask around, then? See if you can find anything out? A local person can get information more easily than a stranger."

"I'm not gonna promise you anything. I'll think about it, okay?"

"Fair enough."

She stood and shrugged into her coat. "It's late and I've got to go to work in the morning."

Glancing at the clock, he saw that his twenty minutes had stretched into an hour while they talked. Their coffee sat, cold and forgotten, on the table. Behind the counter, a waitress glared at them while she noisily refilled napkin holders and ketchup bottles. Tossing a ten-dollar bill on the table, he stood and followed Lacy from the restaurant.

The night was clear and cold. Thousands of stars twinkled in the sky above them, and when he spoke, his breath trailed up to meet them. "Can I call you?"

"No."

"Give me a pen, then."

"For what?"

"So I can write down my cell number. In case you ever want to call me."

"I won't."

"Just in case."

With a sigh of impatience, she plucked her cell phone from her purse. "Give it to me, then."

He recited the number and watched as she programmed it into her phone, once again fighting the urge to pull her into his arms and kiss her.

Lying in bed that night, an ache started in his heart, spreading until his entire body was consumed by it. It had been a tough night. All the talk had brought it back, brought him face to face with his guilt.

When Angel's body was discovered in the alley outside the gang's clubhouse, Soy and Johnny assumed it was a message from a rival gang, and all-out war resulted. People got sloppy. They got scared. They started to talk. Chase cracked the case five days later.

Soy Spade and Johnny Red were arrested and the remainder of The Diamondbacks scattered. But the victory had a high price tag. He couldn't stop seeing Angel's eyes, or his lazy smile, couldn't stop hearing his words. He'd fired his gun twice before in the line of duty. But he'd never before killed a man he'd considered a friend.

After his debriefing, Chase's supervisor, Jim Reynolds, requested a meeting in his office.

"You did a good job for us out there," he said.

"Thanks."

"That being said, I'm taking you out of circulation for awhile."

Chase had expected that. A few weeks of desk detail was standard after completing a tough assignment. "All right."

"I'd like for you to get a psychiatric eval. Talk to someone. Help you deal with the shooting."

"I'm fine."

He gave him a level stare. "I've seen a lot of good cops buckle under the strain of U/C work. I think you're right on the edge. I'm recommending a three-month leave of absence. With pay."

"You're punishing me?"

"It may seem that way, Chase, but it's not a punishment. It's a favor. Go to Europe. Lie on a beach somewhere. Drink some cocktails. Come and see me in three months. We'll talk about your future."

Lacy had asked him why he'd come back. He'd only told her part of the truth. His reasons were twofold, partly altruistic and partly selfish. He'd come back to see if Lacy was everything Angel had said she was. He'd come to check up on Tito, to see whether he was in trouble, and if so, to do his damndest to straighten him out. And he'd come to seek forgiveness from them both. In accomplishing these things, he hoped to God he could forgive himself.

Chapter Nine

Chase had no reason whatsoever to think that Lacy would call him. She'd made it pretty clear she wasn't interested. Still, he couldn't help feeling disappointed that she hadn't. He couldn't shake off his uneasy feeling regarding Tito's apparent disappearance. He told himself he was eager for any tidbit of information Lacy might hear at the diner, anything she might think of that would help him to find Tito De la Fuente. His frustration with his silent cell phone had nothing to do with the feelings she'd stirred up in him the night before. Or so he told himself.

His disquieted thoughts wandered back to Angel's brother. *Where are you, Tito?*

He'd gotten up at five o'clock that morning and driven down to the loading docks where Tito worked. In the office, he'd encountered a salty old man wearing a filthy gray sweatshirt. Tito's boss, Lance Coward, he presumed.

"Whaddya need?" the old man barked.

"I heard you might be looking for some help around here."

The man unabashedly looked him over. "What makes you think so?"

"It's just what I heard."

"From who?"

He shrugged. "Friend of a friend."

"Be straight with me, Boy. Or get the hell off my property."

"A kid named Tito."

The old man scowled. "Oh, Tito sent you, did he? Well you can tell Tito not to bother coming back here any more. I mailed out his last paycheck yesterday morning."

"You fired him?"

"And why wouldn't I? Damned kid hasn't shown up for work in two weeks. That kind of help, I don't need. I don't know what's the matter with kids no more. They come and they go around here like the place had a dad-gum revolving door."

"So you're not looking to hire?"

"Not any friend of Tito's, I'm not."

"All right. Thanks for your time."

As he turned to walk away, the old man bellowed, "You can stop back after the first of the year and put in an application, I guess. I might be looking for someone later. Like I said, they come and they go."

"Maybe I'll do that."

He got in his car and drove to the campground, troubled by this latest piece of information.

His work day started with more conflict. Walking into the house, he couldn't help overhearing a heated conversation between Shane and Mick.

"I can't believe you hired Noise Pollution to play at the carnival."

"They've promised to go easy on the heavy stuff, play some Christmas tunes. I think it will be all right."

"No, it won't!"

"Who did you want me to get, Mick? Bruce Springsteen? I had to pull this thing together quickly, and they were the only band available on such short notice."

"Yeah, well there's probably a good reason for that."

"We're done talking about this, Mick. Noise Pollution is popular with the twenty-five and under crowd. They've promised to tone it down for me and the rest of the old geezers. They're playing at the winter carnival. End of discussion."

"Fine. If they're coming, I'm not!" He turned and stomped from the kitchen. Shane started to follow, but Emma laid a restraining hand on his arm. "Let him c-cool off, Shane. I'll talk to him in a little while."

After an awkward, silent moment, she smiled at him. "Good morning, Chase."

"Good morning, Emma."

"I'm sorry you had to witness that little display of teen drama," Shane said. "I don't know what comes over that kid sometimes." He swallowed the last of his coffee and stood. "We might as well get started. I'd like you to help me build a platform for the ice sculptor's exhibit, and we have to cut some giant candy canes out of plywood for Santa's Palace. Mick's friend, Wendy, is going to paint them for us this afternoon. Hopefully he'll get over his tantrum in time to help us string the lights on the vendor's booths."

It was nearly an hour before Mick showed up to help. He worked silently, sulkily, stapling strings of lights atop the vendor's booths while Shane and Chase built the ice sculpting platform. Chase hadn't taken time for breakfast and by noon his stomach shrieked with hunger. He'd planned to stop at the diner for a sandwich and hopefully touch base with Lacy, but Emma insisted he stay for a bowl of the chili she'd prepared. One whiff of the spicy concoction was all the persuasion he needed. He eyed the mountains of cut-out cookies that cooled on the countertop, hoping they were included in the deal.

The seating arrangements were sticky. Emma placed Chase and Shane at each end of the table, with Mick and Wendy seated opposite from one another on either side. The tension between the two teens was as thick as an oil spill.

As Chase emptied his chili bowl, he assessed the situation. Wendy was definitely a high-maintenance kind of girl. The dark hair and make-up and the Texas-sized chip on her shoulder told Chase that Mick had his work cut out for him.

Mick was cool, seemingly indifferent, but the look on his face said it all. God, he'd forgotten how tough it was to be a kid. Watching Mick and Wendy pretend to ignore each other took him back in time, to the ninth grade, when he was in love with Julie Fennel.

Julie was lovely, with big brown eyes, and pale blonde hair that framed her face like a gilt frame accentuates an exquisite portrait. Every boy in the freshman class was in love with her. Too self-conscious to try and talk to her, Chase started sliding notes between the slats of her locker. Silly, sappy notes in which he awkwardly articulated his feelings. One day, to his utter humiliation, he found a sheet of pink stationary wedged between the slats of his own locker. He stuffed it in his pocket, where it sat like a burning coal all day long, until finally, after seventh period, he went into the bathroom and opened it with trembling hands.

I think you're really cute. If it's you that's been putting the notes in my locker, please meet me at Jerry's after school. We could play air hockey. Julie.

The "I" had been dotted with a little heart, Julie's personal signature.

Eighth period seemed to last for hours that day. Meeting Julie Fennel at Jerry's Arcade was unthinkable. For one thing, it was the most popular hangout in town. Everyone would be there, watching from the sidelines as he made a fool of himself. But not answering Julie's summons was just as unthinkable. What kind of fool passed up such a golden opportunity?

In the end, he called Maxine from the pay phone in the school lobby and asked for permission to stay in town. Permission secured, there was nothing to do except shove his hands in his pockets and walk downtown.

Jerry's Arcade sat in the third block of Center Street, a gaudy purple building with blinking neon signs that drew kids like bears to a honey pot. He walked past it three times before finally gathering his nerve. On his fourth time past, he glanced in the oversized window and saw Julie sitting at a table. Their eyes locked, and his courage fled. He walked past again. That time, he kept on going. A few weeks later Julie started dating a football player named Jason Farrell. They eventually married and had three kids. For years Chase regretted that he hadn't walked into that arcade, that he hadn't taken a chance. His fingers unconsciously closed around the silent cell phone in his pocket. Damn, he wished Lacy would call.

•

It was starting to feel like the longest day of Wendy's entire life. She'd been at the Lucys' house for ten hours. Enough was enough, already.

When she'd dropped her off at ten o'clock that morning, Polly had said she'd see her in a few hours. A few hours was all gone now. So where was she?

When she'd arrived that morning, Emma was in the kitchen, and greeted her with a warm smile. "I'm so glad you could come, Wendy. I'm making a pot of chili for lunch. Would you like to start cutting out the ginger bread boys while I finish up?"

She shrugged out of her coat and slung it over the back of a chair. "Sure. But you'll have to tell me what to do."

"You've never made cut-outs before?"

"My mom's not much of a baker. We usually bought our cookies, if we had them at all."

"Well then, you're in for a treat. Cookie baking is the best part of the holidays." She retrieved a huge bowl of dough from the fridge and set it on the counter, then rounded up two rolling pins and a basket full of cookie cutters. Wendy watched as she gathered the dough into a ball, set it on the counter, and dusted it with flour. Within moments she'd rolled the dough out thin and cut out six gingerbread figures, three boys and three girls.

"That's all there is to it. Wanna give it a try?"

"Sure."

She rolled up her sleeves, put on the apron Emma offered, and went to work on the dough. After several failed attempts, she managed to cut out a half dozen lumpy gingerbread boys.

"There now. You're catching on," Emma said.

"I thought the carnival was two weeks away. Won't these get awfully stale?"

"It's a little early, I know, but I wanted to get them cut out and baked ahead. One more thing to cross off my to-do list," Emma said, sliding a sheet of cookies into the oven. "We'll put them in the freezer for now, then I'll pull them out and decorate them the day before the carnival. But we'll frost a couple of dozen for us to eat today."

It was pleasant, working beside Emma in her cozy kitchen. It was the kind of quality time Wendy had longed to spend with her mother, growing up. The kind of bonding her mother never seemed to have time for.

By noon they'd baked several dozen cookies, and Emma had given Wendy free reign in selecting and decorating a plateful. She experimented with colors until she found just the right shades, and had a blast painting intricate clothing and faces on her creations. Everything was going fine until the men came in for lunch.

Mr. Lucy said hello, and introduced her to Chase Alexander, the new campground manager he'd hired. Tall and blond and busting with muscles, Chase was mad cute. He was the kind of guy that makes a girl tongue-tied just by walking into a room. Mick walked past her without a word and sat down at the table while Emma set out bowls for the chili.

"Have a seat, Chase," Emma said. "I thought I'd put you here, on the end."

"I don't want to put you out, Emma. I can go to town and grab a sandwich."

"Don't be s-silly. We've got more than enough."

When they'd finished their chili, Mr. Lucy walked over to the counter and inspected the plate of cut-outs. "These look phenomenal," he said. "What are our chances?"

"I'd say p-pretty good, if you play your cards right."

Wendy couldn't help noticing the way Emma glowed whenever her husband was in the room. She felt a familiar ache start deep inside of her and wondered if she'd ever be lucky enough to find that kind of love.

Emma grabbed up the platter and set it on the table. "Didn't Wendy do a nice job decorating these?"

"Holy cow, these look more like works of art than Christmas cookies," Chase commented. "They're almost too pretty to eat. But I think I can force myself." He winked at Wendy and she blushed, even though he was way older than her.

"Help yourself, Mick," Emma said.

"No thanks." It was the first two words he'd spoken since coming in. And the last. He got up from the table, put on his coat, and walked out the door. He was acting cold. Distant. Not at all like the Mick she used to know. His meanness left Wendy stinging all over, as if a swarm of angry hornets had been let loose inside her soul.

She was still feeling the pain an hour later, as she painted bold red-and-white stripes on the wooden candy canes Mr. Lucy had made. But later, as she worked to create faces on the eight life-sized reindeer, she felt her pain begin to ease. Her art had always had that kind of therapeutic effect on her. As she added a capful of beige to the sable colored paint, her thoughts drifted to the letter that had arrived in the mail the day before. The third one this month. Reading her mother's letters was like coming upon a train wreck. She didn't want to read them, and yet, she couldn't seem to stop herself. She felt her anger build with each word, each new description of her mother's "dorm," her part-time job in the kitchen, the accounting classes she was taking two nights a week. She made it sound as if she were in college, for God's sakes, instead of the State Penitentiary.

The letters all ended the same way, with her mother saying she loved her, and reminding her when visiting hours were. After reading the letters, Wendy tore them to shreds. Her mother could rot in jail, for all she cared. She'd never bothered to be a mother to Wendy, no way was Wendy going to be her pen-pal now. The thought filled her with a curious mix of anger and sadness. She wished she had a friend, someone to talk to about the way she felt. She would have liked to tell someone the truth about her mother.

People knew about the drugs, but that was only part of it. The drugs were the part that finally put her mother in prison, the part Aunt Polly alluded to whenever people asked, to protect Wendy from the rumors, from having strangers know the terrible truth. She would have liked to tell Mick, because he'd been through a rough time with his birth mother, too. Mick would understand. But obviously Mick didn't want to talk to her anymore.

After dinner, she'd made the mistake of approaching him, and been shot down for her trouble. She'd offered to clean up the kitchen, and Mr. Lucy volunteered Mick to help her. They worked without speaking, Wendy stacking the dishes in the dishwasher while Mick wiped down counters. Finally she couldn't stand the terrible silence any more.

"Do you want to go to the arcade later?" she blurted. "I've got, like, ten bucks saved up."

"I've already got plans. I'm going to the movies with Boots." He wrung out his dish cloth and threw it in the sink. "Why don't you call Brandon?"

The pain was as ferocious as if she'd stepped on another hornet's nest. But Wendy was good at holding in her pain. She held it back until she was safely behind the closed door in the bathroom, the faucet running full tilt to hide the sound of her tears.

Now Emma and Mr. Lucy were sitting together on the couch, watching a movie. Wendy sat in a recliner across the room. It was eight o'clock at night, and she was starting to feel mighty uncomfortable.

Her thoughts were a jumbled mess, thoughts of Mick and Brandon and her mother all tangled up together. A song she'd written played over and over in her mind. Up until today, she'd been wishing she'd torn it from her notebook before giving it to Brandon. It was too personal, too real. But sitting there in Shane and Emma Lucy's living room, an outsider looking in on the kind of life her mother could have provided, but never bothered to, rage overtook her again and she was glad she'd given Brandon her song. Her words. Her truth. It tumbled around in her head, making her dizzy.

... Time after time
I cried n I cried
Year after year
I tried n I tried
to stop the tears
One as they fall,
but millions they came,
what hurts the most
is that u r not ashamed
That U lied. That U left me
Black and black and blue. How could u ...?
Tell me how am I supposed to believe
In u or anything when
u lied 2 me
How am I supposed to trust
U or anyone cause
U lied 2 me.
Cause u lied ulied uliedulieddulied 2 me ...

Her words, her truth. Written for her mother. And for Mick. And for everyone else she'd ever foolishly counted on to care about her.

Chapter Ten

It was three o'clock on Monday afternoon when Lacy finally called. Chase was in the rec hall, repairing some loose planking on the dance platform, when his cell phone vibrated in his pocket. Flipping it open, he saw a number he didn't recognize.

"Hello?"

"I think Tito's in trouble."

Her voice, hushed and breathy, gave him goose bumps. "I'm all ears."

"So are a lot of other people."

The muffled conversation and distant clatter of dishes told him she was calling from work.

"Can we meet later?" he asked.

"I get off at four. We can meet at five. I'll tell you all I know. It's not much."

"Same diner?"

"My apartment. Less ears."

He asked for her address, though they both knew he already knew it. His first order of business, after returning to Sunset Cove, had been to obtain home addresses for both Tito and Lacy. It was basic detective work. One phone call had done it.

He left work at four o'clock and drove to her apartment building, a four-story red-brick building that had definitely seen better days. The elevator was out of order, so he climbed the three flights of stairs. Finding apartment 408, he knocked loudly on the door. She opened it immediately, still wearing her waitress uniform.

"Hey," he said.

"Come on in." She moved aside and he stepped into a small, square living room. A threadbare sofa dominated one wall, with two mismatched chairs and a small TV stand occupying the other. A beat-up coffee table overflowed with cook books and magazines. The space was shabby, but clean.

"It's not much, but it's home," she said, as if reading his thoughts. "Do you want a beer?"

"Sure."

He followed her down a narrow hallway, past a small bedroom and an even smaller bathroom. The kitchen was the largest room in the apartment, and definitely the one she spent the most time in. His glance took in the gleaming cookware that hung suspended from a rack above a butcher block island, the state-of-the-art gadgets that crowded the countertops and the cook books that spilled from every corner. He remembered then that Angel had mentioned her passion for baking.

She opened the fridge, retrieved two bottles of beer, and handed him one. "The story is that Tito's gone missing. No one's seen him in almost two weeks."

He twisted the cap off his beer and took a swallow. "Any idea why?"

"I heard there was a guy looking for him. Big guy. Latino. Word is Tito's hiding out somewhere." She twisted the cap off her beer and tipped the bottle to her lips. "I hope so, anyway."

"I asked around down at the docks. He hasn't been at work."

"I can show you where he lives."

"I know where he lives."

"Maybe we should swing by there. See if he's around."

An inquiry into Tito's address had come back to a seedy motel on Caraway Avenue. Chase had stopped by three times, hoping to talk to Tito. No one came to the door. The last time, he'd gone at midnight and found the door to Tito's unit wide open. A check of the inside revealed stale air and rotting food in the refrigerator. The dresser drawers were open, clothes and papers littered the floor. It looked as though Tito had left in a hurry.

"Maybe I'll go and take another look around."

"Let me go with you."

"You shouldn't be seen around there, Lacy. You don't want whoever is looking for him to start looking for you."

"What about you?"

"I can take care of myself."

"We could just drive by, see if the lights are on. I won't go in."

"I don't know."

"I'm going with you, Chase." She faced him squarely; her stance confident, her eyes defiant, and he remembered Angel also mentioning that Lacy had a stubborn streak.

"Fine. But you're going to stay in the car, out of sight."

The winter sun was quickly setting and it was dark when they reached the motel. Chase parked the car in the shadows in a far corner of the lot and turned off the engine.

"It looks pretty dark," Lacy said.

"I'm going inside."

She faced him, one pretty eyebrow raised. "Breaking and entering?"

"I'm not going to break anything. Much."

"Try and be quick about it. I don't like this place."

"Neither do I. Which is why I wanted you to stay home. Keep the doors locked. I'll be right back."

"Be careful."

Walking in the shadows, beyond the reach of the street lamps, he crept toward the motel. Tito's door was closed, but unlocked. He pushed it open and slunk into the darkness inside. Retrieving his pen light from his pocket, he shined its fragile beam across the room. The same dirty clothes and papers littered the floor. The same empty beer bottles and half filled ashtrays cluttered the table. Nothing appeared to have changed since his last visit. Nothing at all.

He was still surveying the scene when he detected the faint but distinct thud of approaching footsteps outside. His cell phone vibrated in his pocket.

"Yeah?"

"You've got company. There's an old man coming your way. He'll be in there in about thirty seconds."

Flipping the phone shut, he bolted into a coat closet. Moments later, the front door opened and closed. There was a soft click, and then the beam of a flashlight cut a path through the shadows.

"H'lo, Tito? Somebody in here?" a voice bellowed.

Keeping his breathing slow and quiet, Chase peered out at the man. He was old, sixty-five, maybe seventy, with shaggy gray hair and rumpled clothing, the stubble of a two-day-old beard peppering his face. He made his slow, shuffling journey around the perimeter of the room, shining the flashlight as he walked. Chase watched as he stopped at the kitchen table, scooped up a handful of change, and stuffed it in his pocket. When the flashlight neared the closet door, he flattened himself against the wall and took more slow breaths, calculating the distance to the front door. It wouldn't take much to get past the old man, if he had to. Still, he'd rather not be seen. The flashlight moved past him, and moments later, he heard the front door close. His cell phone vibrated in his pocket. Lacy.

"Yeah?"

"You're not going to believe this."

"Try me."

"He just padlocked the front door."

"Terrific."

"What'll we do?"

"I think he may have seen me come inside. Take my car back to your apartment before he calls the cops. I'll meet you there in a little while."

"Chase, I don't have a driver's license."

"Take the back alleys. You'll be fine."

"I'm not going to drive your car. No way."

"Lacy, it'll be fine. Now go! I'll see you in a half hour, tops."

He counted to thirty before making his way back down the hallway. In the bathroom, he shined his pen light across the back wall. Its beam illuminated a small window. Maybe sixteen by twenty. It was going to be a hell of a squeeze.

He pulled out his pocket knife and pried off the screen and jimmied the sash until the window popped opened. Shucking off his jacket, he threw it outside. He grasped the sill, heaved himself up and pushed his upper body through. And got stuck. Cursing, he wriggled backwards and landed on the bathroom floor with a thud. He took a breath. Tried again. Jimmying his body sideways, he pushed one shoulder through, and then the other. Ignoring the pressure of the casing against his chest, he propelled the rest of his body through the space. He heard the sound of fabric tearing, and felt a searing pain rip through his right leg seconds before he tumbled onto the pavement beneath the window. Not stopping to assess the damage, he grabbed up his jacket and raced down the alley, his pant leg flapping as he went.

•

By the time Chase showed up at her door, more than an hour later, Lacy had run the vacuum cleaner and straightened the stacks of books and magazines on her coffee table. She'd showered and shampooed the scent of fryer grease from her hair, then changed into a clean pair of jeans and a sweater. She hadn't shopped that weekend. Her refrigerator held two bottles of beer, a gallon of spring water, and a half dozen eggs, so she'd called the Leaning Tower and ordered a pizza with pepperoni and extra cheese. It was sitting on the counter, steaming hot, freshly delivered, when the knock came at her front door.

She opened it wide, and Chase stepped inside, his sheer size shrinking the room. His hair was disheveled, his face smudged with dirt, and his pant leg was split open from his waist to his knee. She sucked in a breath. Let it out. "What happened to your pants?"

"I had to climb out the bathroom window. Caught my pants on a nail on the way out."

"Oh, gosh." Her gaze moved over his ravaged clothing, his irritable expression. The stress of the evening caught up with her, and she giggled.

His gaze was incredulous. "It's really not that funny. These were my best jeans."

"No, of course it's not." She felt another onslaught of giggles coming and turned away, struggling to control herself. "I ordered a pizza."

"Thank you."

She led the way into the kitchen and set the pizza box on the table. She retrieved plates and forks from the cupboard and the two remaining beers from the fridge and set them on the table next to the pizza. That's when she noticed the gash in his leg, the substantial amount of crusted blood smeared across his thigh, and she was immediately ashamed that she'd laughed at him.

"Oh, gosh. You're bleeding."

"It's just a scratch."

"It's more than that, Chase. I'm going to get my first aid supplies."

"Don't worry about it."

But she was already in the bathroom, gathering up alcohol pads, ointment, and gauze. Returning to the kitchen, she gently washed the wound with soap and water, then dabbed at it with an alcohol pad. He winced.

"Sorry."

She unscrewed the cap from the antibiotic ointment, squeezed a generous amount onto her fingertips, and slowly applied it to the gash. The sensation of touching his bare skin was electrifying.

"Thanks for doing this," he said.

"No problem. You should probably get yourself a tetanus shot tomorrow."

"Nah."

She removed a gauze pad from its pouch and placed it across the wound. "Men," she muttered.

"You say that like it's a bad thing."

She tore a piece of tape from the roll. "It sometimes is."

"How so?"

"Answer me this. Why do men always have to be so strong and stoic?"

"I don't know. Why do women always have to be so soft and sweet?"

The question was asked softly. Glancing up, she saw that his face was now inches from hers. For a terrifying moment she was afraid he was going to kiss her. She looked away from him, focusing on the gauze pad. She ripped off a last piece of tape and hurriedly smoothed it across the gauze. "You're all set. Let's eat before our pizza gets cold."

She pulled out the chair across from him and sat down, and then there was nowhere to look except his face. She took a swallow of beer. "Why do you think the old man locked the door?"

"Obviously Tito didn't pay his rent."

Worry fluttered across her heart. Tito was just a young boy when she and Angel were together. She'd always liked his sunny disposition and his gentle nature. "Do you think you'll find him?"

"I'll find him."

His confidence was a total turn on and she felt a blush creep across her face. She quickly dropped her gaze. She bit into a slice of pizza. Chewed. Swallowed. "So how long have you been a cop?"

He helped himself to another slice. "Since I was about four years old."

"Come on."

"It's true. I'll tell you about it sometime."

"And you really grew up here, in Sunset Cove?"

"Right here on Wisteria Lane."

"And then you left."

"The summer after I graduated from high school."

"And now you're back. Working part-time at the campground."

He regarded her for a long moment, his blue eyes seeming to probe the depths of her soul. "For now."

"Because of what happened with Angel?"

"That was part of it."

She rested her chin in her hand, studying him. "What was the other part?"

"Enough questions, okay?"

"Okay."

They ate the rest of their meal without talking. When they'd finished, Lacy folded the pizza box and slid it into the garbage can, then cleared the dishes and the beer bottles from the table and set them in the sink. She filled the sink with warm water and squirted in some soap. One question still nagged at her, so she risked asking it.

"Why is this so important to you? You don't even know Tito."

"I know enough guys like him. If things had turned out differently, I could have been Tito."

She retrieved a dish cloth and used it to scrub a plate. "What do you mean, if things had turned out differently?"

"We started out in the same place."

"Which was …?"

"Poor boys. Throw-aways. I got lucky. I won the lottery of foster moms. Maxie cared for me like I was her own son. She encouraged me to follow my dreams."

Lacy swirled the dish cloth around in the water.

"Kids on the wrong side of the tracks have to have a passion in life," he said. "Something to reach for. Something to get them through. Some become athletes. Some become cops. Some aren't so lucky. Usually those are the ones who have no one to encourage them in their dreams."

His words hit her hard. Behind her, she could feel him take a step closer. When he spoke, he was merely a breath away.

"What got you through, Lacy?"

It was a personal question, one she didn't want to answer. "I wasn't an orphan," she said sharply. "I had a mother."

"But you grew up poor, in a bad neighborhood, the same as I did. Something kept you out of trouble. What was it?"

She shrugged. "I don't know."

"Sure you do."

She rinsed the plates and the glasses and set them in the drying rack, then pulled out the stopper and let the water rush down the drain.

"There was a German lady that lived upstairs from us. Gretchen Kruger. She was the most tremendous baker. On Saturday mornings she'd work with me, teach me how to bake things. I thought … I don't know. Somehow I associated her cakes and pastries with happiness."

"I can understand that."

"Even after the Krugers moved away, I kept practicing. Trying to become the kind of baker she was. I had this crazy idea that some day I'd have my own bakery. I even have the building picked out." She felt angry tears coming and blinked them back. "Every week for the last three years I've bought a lottery ticket, thinking that some day I'd hit big and buy my bakery. Last week some loser named Johnny Schuyler won forty thousand dollars. He bought himself a brand new pickup truck. Three days later he got drunk and totaled it." She lost her battle with her tears. They streamed down her face and she wiped them away with the back of her hand. "Why does some loser get a break when he doesn't deserve it? Why him and not me?"

He turned her to face him, thumbed the tears from her cheeks. "I don't have the answer to that question, Lacy. I wish I did. But I do know you can't give up." He was inches away, his eyes and his lips beckoning. An inner voice shrieked at her to send him away, but badly in need of the comfort he offered, she ignored it. She stood, still and silent, as his lips brushed against hers. Softly, at first, no more than a whisper of a kiss. Meeting no resistance, the kiss deepened, making her insides sing, setting her senses on alert. She forced herself to pull away from him. "This probably isn't a good idea."

"Probably not."

"I think you should leave now."

Disappointment flickered in his eyes. "Can I see you tomorrow, after work? We could have dinner."

"I have to do my laundry."

"Again?"

"Yeah."

"Then we'll have dinner in the Laundromat. Take out. Anything you want."

"I don't know. I'll think about it." She handed him his coat, then folded her arms across her chest, a thin barrier against him and the desire he'd stirred inside her. She wanted him. There was no doubt about it. But then, she'd wanted things all her life that weren't good for her.

As the door closed behind him, she told herself she wasn't going to see him. The next day, or ever again. She was angry. With Chase, for coaxing her secret from her. With herself, for letting him. She'd told him her dreams, knowing he wasn't the kind of man that could make them come true. What was worse, she'd started questioning whether she even still wanted the bakery, whether the disappointment of waiting was worth the wanting. But if not for her dream, she had nothing. And it didn't get much more hopeless than that. All of these thoughts raced through her mind as she stood at the window, watching his tail lights disappear down the street.

Chapter Eleven

The restaurant was private, intimate. The tables were draped with fine linen cloths, and in their centers, cream colored candles flickered in amber sconces, playing off the golden oak woodwork of the walls. A dozen couples occupied the dining room. Busy for a Tuesday night in December, Polly thought, but the tables and booths were tucked away into cozy little corners, situated so as to make it seem as if they were the only two people in the restaurant. The only two people in the world.

Across the table, Sammy smiled at her, and Polly felt a warm blush creep across her face. She wasn't at all sure she'd wanted to come, and now she couldn't imagine why she had. It was awkward, sitting here, with Sammy knowing her secret. Embarrassing.

After her appointment on Saturday, Polly had felt drained, inside and out. But not surprised. A small part of her had known for weeks before she sat in Dr. Logan's office, looking at the x-rays and listening to him talk about hemoglobin and blood counts and lymphocytes that the cancer was back. She'd experienced the telltale signs, the weakness and fatigue, the lumps and bumps beneath her arm pits, and the night sweats. Of course, she'd dared to hope that she was wrong, that she was just run down, overextended, but a CT scan and a biopsy had confirmed her fears. The cancer was back. It was back, and she'd not come out on the other side of it this time. This time, she was dying.

She'd driven aimlessly for awhile, her cellular phone turned off, not wanting to go home, not wanting to talk to anyone. She'd been pulled, as if by centrifugal force, to the meeting house. She'd felt the need to be in her office, to put her things in order. To think about her options, such as they were. She'd been there for nearly an hour, sitting at her desk, staring into space, when Sammy knocked at the front door. She rose woodenly and opened it.

"I saw the lights on and thought I'd better check it out," he said, concern written all over his dear, lovely face. "Is everything all right?"

"Everything's fine, Sam," she said, the lie of her life. "I'm just catching up on some paperwork."

She'd hoped that would satisfy him, would make him go away, but no such luck. He hesitated in the doorway. "Is there anything I can do to help?"

"Thank you, no."

She'd offered him a cup of coffee, because what else could she do, and they sat and talked for another hour. Finally Sammy stood and carried his coffee cup to the sink. "Are you sure you're all right, Polly? You seem rather preoccupied."

To her horror, she burst into tears.

"Hey, now." He drew her into his arms, as gently as a mother embraces a disconsolate child, and Polly allowed herself to rest against his shoulder and draw strength from his kindness. She cried until her eyes were swollen and her soul, dry.

"What is it, Polly?" he murmured. "Please. Tell me what's wrong."

"I can't," she sniffled.

"And why not?"

"Because I couldn't bear your pity, Sam. I really couldn't."

He pulled away, cupped her face in his hands, and his gaze probed deep inside her soul. "Then suffer my friendship. I care about you very much, Polly. Let me help."

It burst out of her like flood waters burst over a dam. She told him about the fatigue and the night sweats. The suspicious lumps she'd discovered in her neck and under arms. And finally, she told him about the scan and the biopsy.

Sammy didn't patronize her. Nor did he waste words on platitudes. "What's the prognosis?" he asked.

"Not good. I'd have six or eight months without treatment. Twelve or fourteen with it."

He'd listened as she outlined her options. Chemotherapy, radiation, and tests, and tests, and tests. He said nothing through it all because there was nothing to say. They'd both been down that long, hard road before. They both knew the devastating effects of the journey. She, all those years before, and he, as recently as three years ago, when his wife, Mary, was diagnosed with breast cancer.

They talked until it grew late, and then Sammy walked her to her truck and made her promise to have dinner with him the following week. And now here she was, at the Seafarer's Restaurant, in her good black dress and the string of Dollar Store pearls she'd bought for the occasion, since the thief had stolen her good ones. She was as nervous as if it were a first date, ordering red wine and a thirty-dollar plate of sea food she knew she wouldn't eat. Sam was trying to make the evening magical, but she was too world-weary to believe in miracles.

"I'm glad you agreed to come out with me tonight, Polly," he said.

"Well, Sir. I'm glad you invited me." She took a delicate sip of wine, her eyes sliding across the room. "But really, Sam. The Seafarer's Restaurant on a Tuesday night? Doesn't that strike you as a bit decadent?"

"It isn't decadence. It's a celebration."

Her gaze snapped back in his direction. "A celebration. Of what?"

"Of life."

She took another long sip of wine. "I see."

"Do you, Polly?"

"I know what you're trying to do, Sam, and I appreciate it. It's just that …"

"That you're still in the denial stage. I understand that." His gaze was earnest, beseeching. "I went through this with Mary. The denial. The anger. The hopelessness. After she was gone, I regretted all of the things we'd always talked about doing, but never got around to. That's part of the reason I asked you to come out with me tonight. I'd like to help you make a list of things you'd like to do. Starting right now."

She raised an eyebrow. "A bucket list, Sam?

"No, not a bucket list. A seventy list." He opened his jacket and pulled out a small spiral notepad and a pen. "I want you to think of seventy things you'd like to do before your seventieth birthday."

"Seventy things? Now that would be a very ambitious undertaking, wouldn't it? As I've told you, I've not much time. A year, at most, with treatment. A few months, without it."

"Then you'll have to stay well for a very long time, won't you?"

He smiled tenderly, and she sat, fighting tears. Because she wanted that. More now than ever before, she wanted to be well. His hand crept across the table and found hers. "We're neither of us spring chickens, Polly. Let's make the most of life. Let's enjoy every moment of whatever time we have left."

She looked into his weathered face, his kind, compassionate eyes, and for a moment, she almost believed that magic was possible. Even so late in the game as this.

•

Wendy was laying on her bed, working on her latest sketch, Tire Swing, when she heard the distant buzzing of the telephone. She ignored the first three rings, wondering why Aunt Polly even bothered with a house phone any more, when a cell was so much easier.

Ring!

She shook her head. Only old people had house phones these days.

Ring!

It was probably one of Aunt Polly's old-hen friends calling to cluck about their bird-brain bluebird meetings.

Ring! Ring!

Whoever it was, they obviously weren't giving up. Maybe it was important, after all. With a dramatic sigh, she pushed herself off the bed and trudged downstairs to answer it.

"Hello?"

"Wendy? Is that you?"

Hearing Dove Denning's voice, she smiled. "Hey, Ms. Denning."

"I was just about to hang up."

"I don't usually answer Aunt Polly's phone. Why didn't you just call my cell?"

"Actually, I was calling to talk to Polly. Is she there?"

"No. I think she's out on a date."

"Really?"

"Yeah. She left here a couple of hours ago with some old guy."

"Interesting. Listen, have her call me when she gets in, okay? I'll be up until eleven or later."

"Okay." A dark thought crossed Wendy's mind. She could hardly bear to think it, let alone put it into words. "You're still coming to get me after Christmas, right?"

"Absolutely."

"Cool." Relief rushed through her. Back in October Dove had promised to let Wendy visit her in Philadelphia over the Christmas break and Wendy had been looking forward to it ever since. She'd scoured the Internet for places to go, things to do, while in the big city. She wanted to browse in the vintage clothing boutiques on South Street and take in a concert at the International House. She wanted to sample one of the city's famous Philly cheesesteaks. But mostly, she was looking forward to spilling her guts to someone she trusted. And right now, the closest thing she had to that person was Dove Denning. Dove was special. Not just because she was beautiful and had psychic powers. Because she was Dove.

"How's school going?" Dove asked.

"Okay."

"Are you keeping your grades up?"

She crossed her fingers. "More or less."

"How's everything else?"

Terrible, she thought. But that conversation was better saved for when they were face to face. "Fine," she said.

After a few more minutes of small talk, she hung up the phone and returned to her sketch pad, wondering what Ms. Denning could want to talk to Aunt Polly about.

Her aunt was acting strange lately, all weird and quiet. At least she'd let Wendy stay home alone while she went out on her date. She scowled. An old lady on a date. Did it get any freakier than that? Grabbing a fresh pencil, she sketched a few wildflowers into the straggling weeds around the tire swing. She sat back to study the effect. Not bad, she thought.

The drawing stemmed from a memory of one of the few happy days she could remember spending with her mother. It was her birthday. Her mother had packed a picnic lunch of tuna fish sandwiches and potato chips and they'd taken the bus across town to Chapman Park. The city had cleared the lot in the early 1970s and put in slides, monkey bars, and swing sets. On summer afternoons the neighborhood mothers would visit together while their children played. By the 1990s the park had been taken over by drug dealers and the mothers stopped taking their children and the city abandoned the space and the park fell into disrepair. By the year 2000 the park was nothing more than an overgrown lot with a few sagging benches and a handful of ancient sycamores and a tire swing. It was there that Wendy and her mother spread out their blanket and ate their picnic lunch. Later Wendy played for hours on the tire swing while her mother napped in the sunshine. Back home that night there had been chocolate cupcakes and a charm bracelet beside Wendy's dinner plate. It had been one of the best days of her life.

Hearing the front door open, she put away her sketch pad and pencils and went downstairs. Aunt Polly was taking off her coat, and she turned when Wendy entered the foyer.

"Waiting up for me?" she asked, her tone brighter than Wendy had heard it in days.

"No. Just drawing." She watched as Polly hung her coat in the closet and smoothed her dress. "Did you have fun?"

"It was a lovely evening." For a moment she hesitated, as if she might add something. Changing her mind, she turned and walked into the kitchen.

"What did you have to eat?" Wendy asked, not so much interested in the answer as enjoying the unexpected shift in Polly's mood.

"Swordfish, actually."

"Yuck."

"It was delicious." She opened the cupboard and took out a cup, then retrieved a fresh bag of Earl Gray tea from her stock. "Care to join me?"

It was an invitation Polly extended nightly. "No thanks."

"If your homework is done, you should probably think about heading to bed. It's nearly ten."

Wendy groaned inwardly and resisted the urge to roll her eyes. She had to be the only kid in the junior class that had to be in bed by ten o'clock on weeknights. "I'm going right now. Oh. Ms. Denning called for you."

Polly glanced at her in surprise. "She called for me?"

"Yep. About an hour ago. She wanted you to call her back."

"It's rather late."

"She said she'll be up until eleven."

"All right." She filled the tea kettle with water and warmed it on the stove. "Good night, Wendy."

"Good night Aunt Polly."

•

When she'd finished making her tea, Polly carried it to the living room and sat down in her recliner. She leafed through her address book, stopping at the page where she'd written Dove Denning's phone number. She was more than a little curious as to the reason for the call. She knew Dove phoned Wendy every couple of weeks, but she'd only called Polly once, in early November, to confirm the dates for Wendy's visit to Philadelphia. She hoped Dove hadn't changed her mind about that. The girl was looking forward to getting away, and truth be told, Polly was eager for a bit of breathing room. Squinting at the number, she dialed the phone. Dove answered on the second ring.

"Hello?

"Hello, Dove?"

"Hello, Polly."

"Wendy said you called this evening. Is everything all right?"

"Actually, I called to ask you the same question. How are you feeling these days?"

Polly hesitated. "Why do you ask?"

"I don't mean to alarm you, Polly. I didn't know whether I should even call at all. But I've been feeling concerned about your health."

"I see." Dove was a lovely girl, deep-feeling and compassionate. Polly knew that she had extra-sensory gifts. Perhaps she'd had some sort of vision regarding the cancer. "Any special reason?"

"I've been having dreams. Vague impressions."

"About me?"

"Yes."

After a long pause, she said, "There are..." her voice caught. "There are some issues. Some serious issues."

"I'm so sorry. Is there anything I can do for you?"

"I'm working through the emotional aspects. My biggest concern is Wendy. Sooner or later arrangements will have to be made."

"Have you mentioned any of this to her?"

"Not yet."

"Dusty and I have talked. We want you to know that we'll do all we can to help out. When the time comes."

"I appreciate that, Dove. More than you could know."

"Dusty and I will be there on the twenty-seventh. We'll talk more then. But call me any time you need a shoulder, okay?"

•

As Polly set the receiver back in its cradle, Wendy crept back up the stairs and into her bedroom, quietly closing the door behind her. She sank down on her bed, numb with disbelief. She'd only heard one side of the conversation, but one side was enough. Now she knew why Aunt Polly had acted so strangely, lately. It was worse than she'd thought. Much, much worse. Polly wasn't merely irritated or annoyed. She'd finally had enough. Aunt Polly had finally given up on her.

Arrangements will have to be made …

She choked back a wave of nausea and told herself she didn't care. She hated it here anyway. She took out her pencil and her sketch pad. Flipping it open to the Tire Swing drawing, she quickly made adjustments, made the drawing a more accurate picture of how the day really was, instead of how she would have liked for it to be. She drew dark, angry clouds in the sky above the playground, and sprinkled in fat drops of rain; representations of the fear and the sadness she'd felt that day. Because her mother wasn't dozing in the sunshine. In fact she wasn't even there at all. Five minutes after arriving at the park, she climbed in a rusty old pick-up truck with a creepy looking man and drove away, leaving Wendy alone with her tire swing and her tuna fish sandwich.

She scribbled in more clouds, until they completely blotted out the sun. Then she tore the picture into pieces and threw it in the waste basket.

Chapter Twelve

On Tuesday evening Lacy flipped halfheartedly through the pages of the brand new copy of Just Desserts that had arrived in the mail that afternoon. She waited impatiently for the magazine each month, and normally read it from cover to cover the day it arrived, eager for the fabulous hints and exotic recipes it offered. But today she flipped past recipes for Brandied Berry Compote and Hazelnut Pavlova with barely a glance. She couldn't seem to concentrate on the recipes. She couldn't seem to concentrate on anything at all.

She'd texted Chase from work earlier that afternoon, saying she couldn't have dinner with him that night after all. She'd told him she had something important to do. The truth was she had nothing at all to do, important or otherwise. Difficult as it was, she was sticking to her resolve not to get involved with him.

The trouble was, she couldn't seem to stop thinking about him, couldn't stop seeing his sexy eyes, or reliving the magic of his kiss. The things he'd said stayed with her, things about growing up poor, about having a passion in life. He'd hit on a truth that resonated deep inside her, summing up everything she'd ever known and believed about life. He was one of the few people that got it.

She sighed. So many people wandered through their existence as if by accident, living only to die without ever having achieved happiness. Or love. But she couldn't seem to ignore the small inner voice that nagged at her, insisting that love was overrated. And dangerous. If she'd learned anything from her relationship with Angel, it was that.

Staring out her kitchen window, she watched daylight fade to night and thought about passions. Passions were what made life worth living. Taking a breath, she repeated her affirmations.

I will have my bakery one day. I will be outrageously successful, tremendously wealthy.

She tried to envision herself performing the day to day operations of running her business, tried to be a vessel for positive energy, but her heart just wasn't in it.

Oh, get a grip, Lacy! Her inner voice scolded.

She couldn't just sit around moping and wasting time. She needed to do something. Bake something. Because baking was her one true passion, and nothing stirred her belief in the dream more than creating something delectable. With this decided, she flipped open her magazine to a random page. A glossy picture of a beautiful Raspberry Linzertorte stared up at her. The picture evoked warm memories of Gretchen Kruger and she smiled. Pushing back her chair, she moved out to her pantry to take stock. As far as dry goods went she was in good shape. Her shelves were stacked with bins of sugar, flour, almonds, and an array of homemade preserves. Her fridge was another story, though. Glancing at the recipe, she jotted down the items she would need and then, feeling reenergized, she pulled on her coat and gloves and left the apartment.

The cold tore through her and she quickened her pace, thankful that Castillo's Market was only a few blocks away. One of the last vestiges of the optimism that had permeated the Sunset Cove community in the late 1940s, Castillo's Market crouched in the center of Arbor Street, stubbornly refusing to be pushed out by the large supermarket chains. The location was convenient for people like Lacy, who didn't own a car. Their prices were decent, even if their selection left something to be desired. But a proper shopping trip would have to wait until the weekend, when she could take the bus into Hope Haven. For tonight, Castillo's would have to do.

Stepping inside the store, she picked up a shopping basket from beside the door and strolled to the dairy isle. She selected a quart of milk, a pound of butter and a dozen eggs, then moved to the bins of produce in search of a lemon. Selecting the largest lemon they had, she picked it up and sniffed it for freshness. She spent a few minutes inspecting the bright red tomatoes and the fresh cloves of garlic. She hadn't been eating right, lately. It had been ages since she'd prepared homemade tomato sauce. A check of their prices made her wince. When had groceries gotten so ungodly expensive? She started to walk away, but then remembered that one of the keys to positive thought power was to follow her hunches, to act wealthy, and thereby attract wealth. It was worth a try, she decided. And besides that, her mouth was watering for rigatoni with homemade sauce. Dropping the items into her basket, she made her way to the front of the store.

As she took her place in line at the counter, her glance moved idly to the oversized window. A soft gasp escaped her and she squinted again, certain she couldn't be seeing what she thought she was seeing. Two men stood on the corner across the street, speaking animatedly to a teenaged boy on a bicycle. They spoke passionately. She could practically feel their tension from across the street. As if they were trying to coerce the boy into something. Or recruit him, she thought, an icy fist clutching her insides. The boy sat, his arms draped across his handlebars as he listened to them, intermittently shaking his head. Lacy watched as an older, larger Latino man scribbled something on a piece of paper and handed it to the boy. Again, he shook his head. The younger man spoke then. Lacy could see the tension in his stance, the intensity in his eyes. Warm, brown, familiar eyes. Tito's eyes.

She tore her gaze from them only long enough to pay for her items, but in the next glance, she saw the boy wad the paper, tossing it over his shoulder as he sped off on his bicycle. It blew away down the street, and Tito and the other man stood, watching after it as the wind picked it up and carried it into the gutter.

By the time she left the store, Tito was gone. She gazed at the empty street corner and shuddered. She knew most of the people in the neighborhood and could identify the local drug dealers by sight, if not by name. Tito's partner was new to her. Glancing left and right, she hurried across the street and down to the corner, where Tito and the other man had disappeared. Not seeing them anywhere, she turned and made her way back down Arbor Street, toward home. A half a block away from Castillo's Market, she spied a wadded ball of paper lying in the gutter. Picking it up, she opened it and carefully smoothed out the wrinkles. An address she wasn't familiar with was scribbled across it. Tucking it into her coat pocket, she hurried on.

By the time she arrived home she was shaking. She felt relieved for the boy on the bicycle. He'd escaped, for now. But how many other young boys had fallen into the big man's trap? Tito, obviously.

She set her grocery bag on the counter and groped in her purse for her cell phone. As much as she didn't want to get involved with him, she'd better call Chase and tell him what she'd seen.

Chapter Thirteen

On Wednesday afternoon Chase finished up at the campground and headed home to get cleaned up. As it turned out, he was seeing Lacy tonight. She'd texted him yesterday afternoon, saying she couldn't have dinner with him after all. She gave him some lame excuse, but the message was clear. It was the brush-off treatment. Then she'd texted him twice later that night, asking him to call her. Call it pride. He didn't.

She'd called him early that morning and left him a voice mail asking him to get in touch as soon as possible. It was starting to feel a like the jerk-around treatment, and he seriously questioned whether having a woman in his life was worth the aggravation. He waited until two o'clock, when she normally took her break, then punched in her number.

"Hello?" Her voice was breathless, anxious.

"Hey."

"I was starting to think you were ignoring me."

"Just busy. What's up?"

"I saw him."

"Excuse me?"

"I saw him. Last night."

His heart constricted as her words sank in. "Where?"

"Right here, in Sunset Cove. On Arbor Street."

"No kidding."

"I've got something you might be interested in."

He smiled. Of that he had no doubt. "Can I come by later?"

"I get off at six."

"Should I eat first, or do you want me to get something?"

"Actually, I'm making rigatoni. We could have that. Unless you don't like it."

"That would be fine."

"Great. Then I'll see you later. Around seven?"

"See you then."

Clicking off the call, he smiled. Rigatoni was his favorite meal.

•

At six-thirty Lacy lifted the cover of her crock pot and stirred the tomato sauce that had been slow cooking since morning. She tasted a spoonful. Satisfied with the flavor, she re-covered the pot and went to freshen up.

Stepping from the shower ten minutes later, she donned a pair of faded jeans and her favorite turquoise sweater. She brushed her hair and reapplied eye shadow and mascara. As an afterthought, she applied a drop of Opium perfume to each of her wrists. She smiled as its fragrance drifted up to her. She normally only wore Opium for special occasions, and tonight definitely didn't qualify. Not wanting to discuss the big man or the strange address over the telephone, she'd asked Chase to stop by this evening. And since she'd been wanting to make rigatoni anyway, it only seemed right to invite him to have dinner with her. There was nothing more to it than that.

A good night's sleep had done wonders for her outlook, and as she washed a head of lettuce for a tossed salad, she recited her affirmations with renewed energy. Very soon, I will have my own bakery. I will have my own bakery very soon. She allowed herself to envision the sign, A Taste of Heaven: Out of this world pastries!, allowed herself to see the dream, to feel it with everything inside of her. By the time Chase arrived, a little after seven, she was brimming with positive energy, confident she could do anything. Including warding off her feelings of attraction for him.

He walked in, sniffed the air. "Something smells fantastic."

"Let me take your coat."

He shrugged out of his jacket, exposing a black tee shirt that showed off his finely sculpted abs. Despite her resolve, her pulse quickened. He'd brought a bottle of wine, and carried it to the kitchen and stowed it in the fridge.

"Everything's about ready," she said.

"What can I do to help?"

She put him to work slicing a tomato for the salad while she boiled water for the pasta.

"How was work?" he asked.

She told him about her day, her back to him, avoiding eye contact. Her stomach fluttered like butterflies on steroids. What on earth had made her think this was a good idea? Reminding herself that dinner was just an afterthought, she quickly brought the conversation around to the point of the evening.

"So I went down to Castillo's Market last night, and there was Tito, standing on the corner across the street."

"Was he alone?"

"No, he wasn't. He was with this big Latino dude, bald head, some sort of tattoo on his neck." She went on to tell him about the boy on the bicycle, the crumpled scrap of paper. "I don't recognize the address," she said, handing it to him. "It's definitely not in the Cove. Does it ring any bells for you?"

He set his paring knife aside and studied the paper. "Beacon Street." He shrugged. "Hope Haven, maybe."

The water boiled, and she dumped in a half a box of rigatoni.

"Just be careful, okay?" he said.

She turned to face him. "What do you mean?"

"If you should see the big guy again, don't talk to him. Don't even look at him. Just get the hell out of Dodge."

"What about you? What are you going to do?"

"I'm going to find out what his deal is. If I don't like what I find out, I'm going to take him down." He went back to slicing his tomato.

"How are you going to do that?"

"Don't worry about it."

"I'm not worried about it," she said, her stomach clenching with the lie. She'd spent her whole life avoiding trouble. The thought of Chase going in search of it was more than she could fathom. "Just curious."

"I'm gonna go down to Hope Haven after work tomorrow and check out this address." He folded the paper and shoved it in his pocket.

"I want to help you take him down. What can I do?"

"You can stay out of it. It's too dangerous."

"It's too dangerous for you, too. And you're not staying out of it."

"I told you, I can take care of myself. Your pasta's boiling over."

Pulling on an oven mitt, she removed the pot from the stove and dumped its contents into a colander. A cloud of hot steam rose up, coloring her cheeks, disguising the angry flush that had tinted them. Who was he to tell her what to do?

"I'm going with you tomorrow."

He chopped the last of the tomato and dumped it in the salad. "We'll see, okay?"

"No, it's not okay. There's no we'll see about it," she said, feeling supremely annoyed by his condescending attitude. "I've known Tito for a long time. If he's in trouble, I want to try and help him. If you won't let me ride down to Hope Haven with you, I'll take the bus."

He smiled, annoying her further. "Okay, tough guy. But it will be the same deal as last time. You stay in the car, out of sight."

"Fine. But if things go wrong, I'm not driving your car home this time."

He laughed. "Fair enough."

She put the meal on the table and Chase dug in with gusto. Their talk turned to the upcoming winter carnival at the campground and Chase gave her a rundown of the activities Emma had planned.

"They're having an ice skating rink?" she asked. "I haven't ice skated in years. Not since they closed the Civic Center down."

"You should come up next weekend, then."

"I'm not so sure about that." She grinned. "I'd probably fall flat on my face."

"Nothing ventured, nothing gained."

He gazed at her with his sexy blue eyes, leaving her to wonder whether there was any hidden message in his words. "I can't see what benefit there is in making a fool of myself in front of the whole town." She pushed back her chair and stood. "Ready for dessert?"

He cleared his dinner plate from the table, followed her to the sink, and set it inside. "The benefit is, you might actually have some fun, if you'd relax and let yourself. And yes, I am ready for dessert."

Her anger flared again. "Just as an FYI," she said, setting the dessert plate on the table, "I do have fun. All the time."

"Well, I'm glad to hear it." His glance swept over the cake. "What do you call this?"

"It's a raspberry linzertorte."

"A what?"

"A linzertorte. It's Belgian."

He cut a wedge from the center, put it on his plate, and took a generous forkful. "It's delicious."

"Thank you."

He swallowed another bite.

"I do know how to have fun, you know."

"I was kidding, Lacy."

Her face flushed again, and she suddenly felt foolish. As if she gave a rat's behind what he thought. What on earth was wrong with her tonight?

They finished their dessert, and Chase cleared the plates from the table while Lacy filled the sink with water.

"I can get these," she said.

"I'll help you. It's the least I can do."

He stood inches away, rinsing the plates and silver and stacking them in the drainer. His closeness was unnerving. She was acutely aware of his every move, of his cologne, and the brush of his hand against hers. His blatant masculinity threw her off guard and she found herself unable to do more than utter one-word responses to his questions.

"Is anything wrong, Lacy?" he finally asked.

"No."

"You seem kind of quiet all of a sudden. I hope you're not still upset with me."

"Why would I be upset?" she snapped.

"The comment about not having any fun."

"Forget about it."

"Okay."

"I just don't know why you said it. Do I seem that rigid?"

"Not rigid. Maybe a little too serious, at times. But I think you're a great girl."

Her heart fluttered. An inner voice warned her to leave it alone, but she couldn't resist pushing the envelope. "Oh you do, do you?"

"Yeah, I do. You're smart, and determined. Beautiful," he lifted a strand of her hair and tucked it behind her ear, adding softly, "And you smell incredible."

His touch sent shock waves coursing through her veins, setting her survival instincts into overdrive. She pulled the stopper from the sink and quickly backed away from him. "There. All done."

"Would you like to go and sit in the living room? We could talk some more."

For a brief moment, she considered it. But thoughts of sitting on her couch with Chase set a swarm of butterflies fluttering in her tummy. "Let's go for a walk instead," she blurted.

He stared at her as if she'd just grown an extra head. "Are you serious? Lacy, it's sixteen degrees outside."

"A brisk walk is good for the digestion. Very invigorating. Everybody knows that." Before he could protest, she grabbed his coat from the back of the chair and thrust it at him.

Moments later they were walking down Cottage Street, zigzagging their way around the patches of ice that had collected on the sidewalk. "You really do this every night?" he asked. "After you eat?"

"Only sometimes."

Huffing out a breath, he pulled up his collar. "How far do you go?"

"Just a few blocks."

They reached the intersection at Arbor Street and she instinctively turned left. In the third block, her footsteps slowed. It was only for a heartbeat, but he noticed.

"Is this the place?" he asked, gazing intently at the abandoned building between the Penny Pincher Thrift Store and the pawn shop.

"What place?"

"The place you want to buy for your bakery."

"Yeah," she said, suddenly embarrassed, wishing she'd never mentioned it to him.

Wiping a circle of grime from the window, he peered inside.

"You can see it better in the daytime," she said defensively. "I went in and looked at it once. With the realtor. It's perfect."

"Tell me your plan."

"Well, for starters, I'd put in a new counter. Something durable. Maybe granite. With space underneath to display my baked goods. And I'd have café tables for people who want to sit and read, or just visit. I'd sell gourmet coffees. And maybe some of those specialty party dips." She knew she was babbling but found herself unable to stop. "There's a little office out back. I'd do my paperwork out there. And there's even an office upstairs with a separate entrance. I could rent that out to help pay the loan."

"Rent it out to who?"

"I don't know. A lawyer. Or maybe an insurance agent." Spoken out loud, the plan sounded foolish and she turned and started to walk away.

He reached her in three strides. "Sounds like you've got it pretty well planned out."

She shrugged.

"What's the asking price for the building?"

"I don't know," she lied. "I don't really want to talk about it any more."

They walked back to her apartment building in silence. When they reached the door, he said, "Can I come up for a little while?"

"Not tonight."

"Okay." He leaned against the railing. "Then I guess I'll see you tomorrow, after work."

"Great."

"We'll see if we can find out what Tito's gotten himself into."

"Right."

He hesitated. "Can I kiss you again?"

"Better not. I'm catching a cold."

"You don't have to make excuses, Lacy. If you're not interested, just say so."

She took a breath, forced the lie from between her lips. "I'm not interested."

Disappointment flared in his eyes. "That's all you had to say."

"It's not that you're not a good person. It's just ... "

"I got it, okay? I'll see you tomorrow." He pushed off against the railing, jammed his hands in his pockets, and walked away. Watching him leave set a firestorm of conflict blazing inside her.

"I don't know if I am or not," she called softly.

He turned back, regarded her for a long moment. "That's okay, too."

"I'm sorry. I'm being indecisive."

He returned to where she stood. "I'm not asking you to rush into anything here, Lacy. No pressure. Just keep an open mind, okay?"

She smiled. "Okay."

"I'm going to kiss you now, but it doesn't mean a thing, okay?"

"Okay."

His lips were cold at first, and then they warmed beneath the force of physical contact and desire. His arms encircled her and she felt her world melting into his. And it meant everything.

Chapter Fourteen

The next morning, Chase ran the address Lacy had given him through Map Quest. Fourteen Hundred Beacon Street was definitely a Hope Haven address. According to his directions, it wasn't in a very nice section of town, a fact which didn't surprise him in the least. After work, he drove over to Lacy's apartment with serious second thoughts. All at once it didn't seem like such a good idea to take her. But better she go with him than to make good on her threat to take the bus downtown alone. Damn it, this was why he never allowed himself to become involved with anyone. Detective work was dangerous. Especially when he had no idea who he was dealing with.

Not finding an empty spot anywhere on her block, he double parked in front of her building, took out his cell phone, and called her. "I'm out front. Are you ready to go?"

"I'll be right down."

Moments later she came out the front door, and his heart squeezed in his chest. She looked fresh and pretty, a red wool cap pulled over her curls, the winter air tinting her cheeks pink. She looked like a child, an innocent lamb. He hoped to God he wasn't leading her to the slaughter.

She opened the car door, slid inside, and buckled her seatbelt.

"It's not getting any warmer out here, is it?" she said cheerfully.

"No, it isn't."

He was barely able to concentrate on her chatter as he headed down the winding lake road that led into Hope Haven City. His thoughts were troubled, his mind racing. "We're not exactly going to the greatest section of town, so keep the doors locked and try to stay out of sight, all right?"

"You already told me that."

"I'm just reminding you."

Twenty minutes later they reached the city limits. Driving past Hope Haven City School, Chase did a double take. The old brick exterior had been torn off and replaced with a modern stone and glass facade, new windows, and a large addition.

"Looks like they gave the old stomping grounds a face lift," he commented. "I wouldn't have known the place."

She shrugged. "I'm sure it's still the same old dump inside."

The bitterness in her tone caused him to look over at her. She studied her fingernails, barely giving the building a second glance. "It's kind of funny, to think we both walked those halls and our paths never crossed. What year did you graduate?"

"I didn't graduate. I quit."

"Oh."

"Leaving that place was like finally waking up from a bad dream."

"I'm sorry."

She shrugged. "It doesn't matter now."

A few blocks from the school, he noticed the glow of neon lights and slowed again. He stared at the arcade. "I can't believe this place is still here."

"It comes and goes. It's probably changed hands a dozen times since you were in school."

Studying the sign, he saw that it was no longer called Jerry's. The flashing neon lights spelled out *Atomic Video Arcade—it's da bomb!* Judging from the crowd of teenagers milling around outside, it was still the most popular hang out in town.

As they neared their destination, the scenery changed dramatically. The trendy shops gave way to tired, unkempt buildings, garbage collecting in the gutters. He took a left onto Beacon Street and cruised slowly past number Fourteen Hundred. A half block away, he pulled into a parking spot and studied the building. Short and squatty, it sat jammed between two larger buildings, both of them abandoned. Its dirty white clapboard was barely visible beneath the graffiti tattooed over every inch of its surface. There were symbols and numbers, names of gangs. In the midst of the profanity, a large cross fought for space, the words John 3:16 written across its beam. Out front, a pair of teenaged boys played hackey sack, cigarettes dangling from their lips.

"Nice place," Lacy said.

He faced her. "You're going to wait for me right here, right?"

"Right."

"Keep the doors locked. I'll be back as quick as I can."

As he opened the door, she reached across the seat for his arm. "Be careful."

"I will."

Jamming his hands in his pockets, he approached the building. The boys looked up from their game.

"Hey, dude," he said, addressing the older, dark-skinned one.

The boy looked him over for a moment, nodded, and went back to his game.

Chase gestured toward the building. "What goes on in here?"

The boy shrugged. "Ow know, man."

Chase stepped up to the door and turned the knob. It was unlocked. He pushed his way inside, finding himself in a small, dark hallway. It was dank and sour smelling. Another door led to a large, empty space with cinderblock walls and a battered hardwood floor. His glance moved across the room, seeking clues in the shapes huddled against the walls, covered by tarps. Lab equipment? he wondered. Probably this was some sort of gang club house. Or maybe it was simply a dead end. On the back wall he saw a small window covered with chicken wire. Hearing muffled shouts, he walked toward it and peered out. The lot out back was surrounded on three sides by a chain link fence. The pavement was cracked and uneven. In its center a tall length of PVC pipe supported a basketball hoop. A handful of men laughed and jeered as they dribbled, took aim, and shot. Chase scanned the small crowd, looking for a big Latino with a tattoo. There was no sign of him. Most of the players were in their late teens or early twenties, most of them Latino. Any one of them could have been Tito De la Fuente. Deciding to see what was under the tarps, he turned and walked toward them.

He hadn't heard the man's footsteps, hadn't heard any sound at all, but as he reached for a corner of a tarp, a thick, gravelly voice demanded, "What are you doing in here?"

He dropped his hand to his side and slowly turned around. A middle-aged man stood in the doorway, his arms folded across his chest. A large, Latino man wearing a pair of blue work pants and a sweatshirt. Chase's glance moved across the tattoo on his neck. He willed his body to relax.

"I think I'm in the wrong place. I'm looking for the DMV."

The muscles in the man's arms flexed slightly. "The DMV's clear across town, on Lexington. But it closes at four."

Chase smiled. "My luck."

The man nodded toward the window. "You play basketball? We might be looking for a center."

"Never been a fan."

The man's suspicious gaze fixed on Chase's face. "What are you really here for?"

Sizing him up, Chase calculated that the man had a good fifty pounds on him. Two hundred fifty pounds of solid muscle that stood between him and the front door. Dude seemed fairly relaxed, but he could just be playing it cool. Knowing it could go either way, Chase took a chance. "I'm looking for a kid named Tito."

The man's face gave nothing away. "What do you want with Tito?"

"I have some news for him. About his brother."

His face remained impassive, impossible to read. "He's not here. Haven't seen him all day."

"Do you know where he hangs out?"

"Come back tomorrow night. You can talk to him then."

"I'll do that." He turned and walked out, past the tarps and the window, past the big Latino man, his nerves jumping with every step.

The air outside was a welcome relief after the dank, dark room. He stood on the sidewalk, filling his lungs, trying to think. He turned back and looked at the building, listened to the sounds of the men out back playing basketball. It was early. They had to do something to fill their down time. They were some sort of street gang, no doubt, but something wasn't jibing. He felt like there was something he was missing. He also felt like he was being watched. He glanced up and down the street, into the windows of the empty buildings, watching for movement, seeing none. If the men playing basketball were part of a gang, then their leaders had to be close by. Chase was sure that by now, he was aware there was a stranger poking around, asking questions. Wherever the ring leader was, he was biding his time, watching. Waiting.

For tomorrow night? he wondered.

He thought fleetingly of the stories Max used to tell him of the Great Horned Owl. How it blended with the shadows of the forest until dusk, when it would spread its wings and fly, gliding silently through the dark woods, its eyes gleaming like amber spotlights in the dark. Silent and swift, no brush of wings to alert his unsuspecting victims of his approach, of certain death.

Like the Great Horned Owl, drug dealers were predators. They hunted the streets at night, feeding off the fear and weakness of their prey. They were very good at what they did. He hoped to God he was better. One thing was for certain. He was being set up for something. And when he came back tomorrow night, he'd be coming alone.

He headed back to the car, troubled that he'd made some big mistakes. He'd gotten sloppy. Gotten caught. "The DMV," he muttered. "Outstanding, Alexander."

He reached the car and Lacy unlocked the door and pushed it open, her expression eager. "Did you see Tito?"

"I don't know what he looks like." He climbed in, shut the door, turned the key. "I saw a lot of guys that could have been him, though."

"Really? What were they doing?"

He put the car in gear and tapped the gas. "They were playing basketball."

"Playing basketball? For real?"

"Yup."

"So what do we do now?"

"Go home. A guy told me to come back tomorrow night, but I'm pretty sure it's a dead end." He pulled out into the flow of traffic. Along the sidewalks, kids were hanging out. Boys leaned against buildings, smoking cigarettes while young girls pranced around in short skirts, though it was barely thirty degrees outside. He felt strangely depressed, remembering long lost days when Maxine had brought him and his brothers down here for dentist appointments and school clothes shopping. That seemed like another world, now.

"When did this town get so run down?"

"This section has always been run down. You just don't remember it because you've been away for a few years."

He thought about memories, how they colored people and places, made them seem gentler than they'd really been. God. He must be getting old.

"What time are we coming back tomorrow?" Lacy asked.

"We're not. I am letting it go."

"Are you kidding?"

He shrugged. "I told you, it's a dead end. We're not going to find anything out by hanging around down here."

"But what about Tito?"

"Whatever Tito may or may not have gotten himself into isn't my problem."

"So you're just going to forget about him?"

"That's right."

She was quiet for a moment, then said, "Okay. If that's how you feel."

"That's how I feel."

She went quiet again, and he drove for a few blocks, hoping he'd convinced her. Finally, she said, "Well, as long as we're down here, I have an idea."

He shot her a sideways glance and saw that her eyes twinkled mischievously.

"What's your idea?"

"Let's go in that arcade."

"The Atomic Bomb?"

"Yeah. Let's go in."

"Are you serious?"

"We could play some games. Have some serious fun."

He heard the subtle challenge beneath her words and he got it. "Is this about what I said last night? Because if it is, you don't have to prove anything to me, Lacy."

"I'm not trying to prove anything. Except maybe that I can kick your butt in air hockey."

He smiled. "Think so?"

"I know so. I used to work at a video store. We had a table out back. We played when it was slow. Nobody could beat me."

"Well Lady, I hate to tell you this, but you've just met your match."

"Loser buys dinner."

"You're on."

He pulled into a spot in front of the arcade and they got out. Inside, the building was a hot mess of blinking lights and automated sounds. A throng of teenagers parted to let them pass and Chase felt subtle vibes of disapproval radiating from them. For the second time that night, he felt old.

"Maybe this wasn't such a good idea. We're the only people over seventeen in the place."

"You're never too old for air hockey. Look, we've got the table to ourselves."

His glance was drawn to a gloomy corner, where an air hockey table sat like a lonely dinosaur amid the fancy electronic wonders. He put two quarters into the slot and turned it on. The machine hummed and came to life with a soft whoosh of air and they took up their paddles.

Lacy was relentless. Highly competitive. She raced back and forth, hair flying, that deep, throaty laughter he loved caressing the air around him as she battered the plastic hockey puck with her paddle. Chase forgot about feeling like a senior citizen as they played like children. His old regrets over Julie Fennel melted away, and he thanked whatever magic genie had granted him this do-over.

They played six games. In the end, she beat him five to one. They were still laughing as they climbed into his car.

"Okay, where to?"

"Just drive. We'll eat at the first place we see. It'll be more fun that way."

Her eyes were sparkling again and he smiled, liking this new, lighthearted Lacy. After several blocks, she exclaimed, "Right there, on your left!" and he made a quick turn into the parking lot of a Bob's Big Boy Restaurant.

"Good God. You mean to tell me this place is still here?"

"Looks like."

He stared in amazement at the familiar red-and-white striped roof, at the iconic six-foot statue out front. "I can't believe it's still in business. We used to come here every Saturday. My foster mother would bring us for lunch after grocery shopping."

"No kidding."

Inside the restaurant they were greeted by the smells of frying burgers and rotisserie chicken. Chase noted that the same red-leather booths he remembered from his childhood lined the walls, the same black-and-white linoleum covered the floors.

"It's nice to see that some things haven't changed."

They placed their orders at the counter. Chase paid for the burgers and fries and the counter attendant, a girl of about sixteen, handed him a buzzer. He carried it to the corner where he and Lacy slid into a booth.

Lacy played with a napkin holder. "What do you suppose Tito and the big guy were doing in the Cove?"

"I don't know."

"They seemed so intense, talking to that kid. I could feel the tension from across the street."

"If they're part of a drug gang, maybe they were out looking to recruit some fresh dealers. Believe me, cops get used to seeing the same faces after awhile."

She set the napkin holder down, her eyes looking intently into his. "You really hate them, don't you."

"I hate what they do to kids, to communities. The destruction. That's part of the reason I became a cop. To try and stop the flow of crime. Or at least, slow it down to a trickle."

His buzzer buzzed, and he walked to the counter to retrieve their orders, grateful for the distraction. He'd have to change the subject quick, get her mind off of Tito and the ugly white building on Beacon Street.

"Oh my God," she exclaimed, eyeing the oversized burgers and the mountainous tray of fries. "We'll never eat all that!" She picked up a French fry and took a dainty bite. "Speaking of crime stopping, you were going to tell me a story about how you became a cop when you were four years old."

He picked up his burger, took a bite. "I will. Sometime."

"Why not now?"

"I'm not sure you really want to hear it."

"Try me." She propped her chin in her hand, gazing into his eyes again. "Tell me your story, Chase. Let me know you."

He was starting to feel more than a little uncomfortable. It wasn't a time in his life he liked to dwell on, and the story wasn't one he often shared. And never with beautiful girls he was trying to impress.

"It's nothing, really. Just that I used to like playing cops and robbers when I was small. I had a little tin gun with a plastic handle. Slept with it under my pillow at night. No big deal."

Her expression was one of disappointment. He knew she didn't believe him, not for a minute, but he was grateful to her for not pressing. He thought it was a done deal, but driving home later, she said softly, "Why don't you trust me?"

His hands tightened on the wheel and he stared at the road ahead. "I do trust you."

"But you won't share anything real with me. Even though I told you about my dream of owning a bakery. I've never told anyone that before."

He felt a pressure building inside of him. He wasn't a man who liked to share the unsavory details of his past. He was much more comfortable living in the here and now. But her disappointment clung to him, permeating the air he breathed, erasing the magic of the evening they'd shared. He could hardly bear the weight of her silence, still, he drove without speaking, out of the city and up the winding road that led to Shadow Lake, his secrets locked up safely inside. He pulled onto Wysteria Lane and drove to her apartment building. As he slid the car into an empty spot out front, she gathered her purse from the floor.

"See you around."

As she reached for the door handle, the pressure inside him built to the bursting point. This was another reason he never got involved with women. Relationships demanded opening yourself up, giving yourself away, piece by piece, until eventually you lost control. But a sixth sense told him if he didn't take the chance she'd get out of the car and walk right out of his life. And that wasn't a chance he was willing to take either.

"My mother had me when she was fifteen years old," he blurted. "My father was twenty-one. They never stood a chance."

She let her hand fall away and settled back into her seat.

"They had no money, no resources. We lived in a rat hole in East Arlington. My father worked every minute of the day trying to get ahead, but they only got farther and farther behind. I remember lying in my bed at night, listening to them fight about money. My mother couldn't work, she had no education. And she had me. My father resented the hell out of that."

The sky was wintry dark. He felt, rather than saw her eyes upon him.

"Every once in awhile I'll have a flash of a memory of my mother. I'll remember her soft hands wrapping me in a towel after my bath, or the sound of her voice, saying my name. But I can't seem to remember having any good times with my father. All I remember is him screaming, and her crying."

She continued to watch him in the dark.

"Finally, to try and please him, she got a job. She worked cleaning office buildings at night. He stayed home with me. It was the worst few months of my life."

"Why?"

"Because he was a monster. He got his kicks out of teasing me, tormenting me. He'd bring me a new toy, hold it out to me, and then snatch it away, just for the fun of watching me cry. It's a terrible thing to do to a kid.

"After awhile, teasing me wasn't enough. He got physical. I remember he'd strap me into my car seat and put me in the shower. He'd turn the cold water on full blast and just leave me sitting there, so cold I thought I'd die."

"Oh, Chase."

"He was savvy. He'd hit the bottoms of my feet with a wooden spoon, where the bruises wouldn't show. The harder I cried, the worse it was."

"Why would he do that?"

"He said it was a tough world, and I had to man up."

"But you were just a little boy."

"It didn't matter. Not to him." He drew a breath. "My mother finally caught on to what he was doing. She was scared to death of him, but her love for me was stronger than her fear. One night, she confronted him. She pointed out the bruises on my feet and accused him of abusing me and he slammed her into the wall and broke her nose. That was enough to finally make her call for help. He went out, and when he came back, the cops showed up. They took one look at my mother's black eye and they slapped a pair of handcuffs on my dad. That moment changed my life."

"How?"

"Up until then, I'd felt helpless, hopeless. But that night—I realized there was a way I could be in control. That badge, those handcuffs, they equated to power. If I could just have them, I could have the power to save myself. To save my mother. The power to make the bad guys go away."

He paused, swept away in his memories.

"The next few days were the best I'd ever known. My mother and I moved into a shelter. She'd play with me in the back yard, and we'd laugh together and there was no shouting, no fear." He pulled in a breath and let it out. "But then my father made bail. He came looking for us. He walked into the yard where we were playing one evening and he beat my mother to death in front of me."

She gasped softly.

"He shoved my face next to her broken body and he said, 'You see this, boy? This is what happens to people who don't keep their mouths shut. This is what happens to narcs. So that's exactly what I became. An undercover narcotics agent. A narc. And every time..." His voice cracked. "Every time I slap the cuffs on some low life, scum-sucking pig, I see his face."

He felt a familiar rage burning inside him. The rage that scared him sometimes, that came from deep down in his soul. The rage that fueled his passion.

"Come here," she said softly. And she held him. "I'm so sorry." He felt the wetness on her face as she cried the tears he couldn't. He was lost in her tenderness, in the sweetness of her perfume, the softness of her touch.

"That's what does it for me, Lacy," he whispered. "That's what gets me through."

•

Lacy lay awake until late into the night, thinking about all of the things he'd told her. She'd wanted to know him, to be trusted with his secrets. But in no way was she prepared for that kind of confession. It changed things. He'd bared his soul to her, and the responsibility of his trust was like an albatross around her neck. Because she was falling in love with him. And she had the scared-sick feeling that loving Chase would be the end of her dream.

Her thoughts drifted to earlier that evening and she frowned, wondering why he'd lied to her about his intentions toward Tito. Knowing him, she knew there was no chance of him letting it go. He was trying to protect her. Returning to Beacon Street would be dangerous. Which was exactly why she wasn't letting him go back there alone. She was a small woman. She couldn't offer much in the way of protection, but she could certainly call for help, if it turned out he needed it. She'd take the early bus, hide out somewhere, see what was going down. She'd do whatever she had to do. There was no telling what she'd be walking into, but there was one thing she knew for certain. Dream or no dream, there was no way she was going to take a chance on losing him, now that she'd found him at last.

Chapter Fifteen

Once she set her mind to it, Polly found she enjoyed making her "Seventy List" tremendously. On Friday morning she sat at her kitchen table with her head bent over the writing tablet Sammy had given her three days before. She'd worked on it steadily, and now, with a flourish, she added item number seventy to her list. Sitting back, she looked it over with satisfaction. Some of the items were preposterous, like number thirty, *See All Fifty States*, and she doubted she would complete them. But others were as simple as making a snow angel, or smelling a spring flower. Those things she could easily accomplish. At any rate, the list gave her some goals to work toward and a renewed sense of purpose. She had the sneaking suspicion that that was Sammy's intention all along.

They'd come up with fifteen items in the restaurant, and he'd made her promise to keep adding to the list. He was stopping by this morning and she felt as excited as a child to show it to him. Her brow creased. He'd told her to be ready by ten. Ready for what, she couldn't imagine.

Since it was barely eight-thirty, she prepared a second cup of tea and lingered at the table, enjoying the peace and the quiet. An hour earlier Wendy had flounced off to the school bus without a word. She'd been sullen lately, more quiet than usual, and Polly could only wonder what the latest bit of drama could be.

As she sipped her tea, Polly's gaze was drawn to a large maple tree in her back yard. She squinted into its branches for a moment, then retrieved a pair of binoculars from a kitchen drawer and adjusted the dials, focusing in on the elaborate empty shell of an oriole's nest high in the treetop. She smiled. The orioles had visited her yard each spring for as long as she could remember and she always looked forward to their return. The splash of orange and black as first the male appeared. The sound of his sweet love song filling the air as his lady friend arrived, a lovely figure in greenish-orange and palest gold. She loved to watch as the female created her nest; a work of art she sewed together with bits of string, plant fibers, hair, strips of paper and cloth, or anything else she could scavenge from the yard, until she'd fashioned them into an elegant silver basket. Truly one of the most amazing cradles made by any American song bird.

When she'd finished her tea, she combed her hair and dabbed on a splash of perfume before pulling her brown sweater from the closet. Then, remembering that item number forty-three on her list was Be More Adventurous, she replaced the sweater on its hanger and selected instead a purple sweater she hadn't worn in years. Trying it on, she was pleasantly surprised to see that it still fit perfectly.

She stood before the full-length mirror and appraised her reflection. The sweater lent a bit of sparkle to her pale blue eyes. Barely worn, the cotton was soft and lovely, and she wondered why it had sat, forgotten, in the back of her closet for so long.

At precisely ten o'clock, Sammy knocked on the front door. Smoothing a wrinkle from her black slacks, she went downstairs to let him in.

"Why Polly, you look stunning," he said, kissing her on the cheek.

"Thank you, Sir." She felt a blush burn across her face. "Would you like a cup of tea?"

"I'd love nothing more." He glanced at his watch. "But I'm afraid we haven't got time."

He stood in the doorway and waited while she gathered up her coat and purse. "So tell me, Sam, what is it you have planned for this morning?"

He grinned. "Number fourteen."

She drew a blank. "Number fourteen?"

"Don't tell me you've forgotten our list? Number fourteen was Do Something Impulsive, remember? You said that just once you wanted to enjoy an outing that you hadn't planned and organized all of the fun out of. Today you're going to cross your first item off your list." Beaming, he handed her a bag. "You'll need this."

She opened the bag and peered inside. Frowned. "A digital camera?"

"That's right."

"I don't understand."

"We're going on a photo scavenger hunt." He removed a folded sheet of paper from his pocket and showed it to her. "I found it on the Internet. We have to go around and photograph these twenty items."

Her glance moved down the list. "Some of these don't look so difficult. But where on earth will we find a hot air balloon this time of year?"

"But don't you see? That's the fun of it, Polly."

They made their way down the winding hill into Hope Haven City, chatting amiably.

"Okay," Sammy said, when they reached the city limits. "What's the first item on our list?"

Polly pulled the folded sheet of paper from her purse. "It says, photograph something old. I wonder if I could take a picture of myself?"

He glanced at her, his expression dubious. "No, that will never do."

"And why not?"

"Because you're the same age as me, give or take, and I am most definitely not old. We'll have to think of something else."

As they drove through the Hope Haven business district, the golden domed roof of the city courthouse loomed from Center Square, both impressive and intimidating at the same time. Sammy pulled into the adjacent lot.

"I believe the court house was one of the first buildings erected in the city. Some time around 1802. That ought to qualify as old, wouldn't you think?"

They got out of the car and Polly set up a shot of the structure, careful to include the date engraved in the cornerstone; July 12, 1802, just as Sam had said. When she'd checked that the photo was clear and in focus, she climbed back into the car, a self-satisfied smile on her face.

"One down, nineteen to go."

The second item on the list was photograph a blue door. Sammy cruised through the city streets, scanning the left-hand side while

Polly checked the right. Within a few blocks they came upon a brick row house, its shutters and doors trimmed in indigo.

"Right there," Polly exclaimed, fumbling for the camera. After taking the shot, she checked the viewer screen and grimaced. "My, what a ghastly combination of colors."

Next on the list was photograph two things that rhyme. After driving several more blocks, Polly spied an old woman hobbling down the sidewalk with a cane. "Slow down!" she cried, surreptitiously photographing the old woman.

Sammy looked perplexed. "I don't get it."

"Two things that rhyme," Polly said, grinning.

"A woman with a cane?"

"Precisely. A lame dame."

Sammy laughed. "My dear, I do believe you're getting into the spirit of this."

He slowed in search of the next item, and after a near miss with a garbage truck, decided to park the car in a city lot and look for the rest of the items on foot. They photographed a wall of graffiti on Lincoln Street, a yellow school bus on North Main. In search of 'something naughty,' they decided on a teenaged girl standing outside a video arcade, smoking a cigarette.

"Do you think she qualifies?" Polly asked.

"I think she's the very picture of naughtiness."

Polly frowned. "She reminds me of my niece."

"Only happy thoughts today, Polly," Sammy said, linking his arm through hers. "What's next?"

"A hot air balloon."

"We'll come back to that one. Next?"

"Something that begins with the letter M. Too easy." She snapped a photo of a mailbox. "Now we have to find a red shoe."

Within a few blocks, they came upon Anderson's Shoe Shoppe. Featured prominently in the window was a pair of glittery red pumps. Polly took a picture. "Oh my, aren't those unusual."

"I think you should buy them."

She hooted. "And wear them where?"

"I don't know. To church?"

"Oh, ho! Wouldn't I be the talk of the town!"

"I think you'd be stunning."

Chuckling, she glanced at the list. "Now I have to photograph someone in uniform."

"The police station's way across town."

"How about a fireman?"

"For that, we'd have to go to a fire. Definitely not my idea of fun. How about him? " He indicated the oversized statue in front of the Bob's Big Boy restaurant across the street.

"I don't know that I'd call it a uniform, exactly..."

"Are you joking? That poor boy's worn those britches for more than fifty years. He's an American icon."

She giggled. "If you say so."

Crossing the street, she took the photo.

"Lord, this brings back memories," Sammy said. "Do you remember the day we came here on a double date?"

"It was most definitely not a date. You and I and James and Martha came here after working on a history project at the library. We were partners, not lovers."

"You remember it your way, Sister, and I'll remember it mine." He linked arms with her again. "Now what's next on your list?"

"Oh dear. It says I have to photograph a kiss."

"Why not kiss the Big Boy? I'll take the photo this time."

"Oh, but I'd feel foolish!"

"Nothing wrong with a little tomfoolery every once in a while. It's what keeps us young. Now pucker up."

Laughing like a child, Polly stepped up to the statue, rose on her tiptoes, and planted a kiss on his weathered chin.

"Very nice," Sammy said, surveying the photo. "What do you say we go in and grab a burger? For old time's sake?"

Polly's glance moved over the restaurant. It had been among the most popular in town back in the day, but now it looked a little on the seedy side. "Are you sure?"

"Why not?"

Polly's hands burned with cold, and the warmth inside the restaurant made the sticky floors and the worn leather booths more bearable.

"It seems to have gone downhill a bit," she said, sinking into a booth with a slightly tilting table.

"I'll bet they still have the best darn burgers in the city. You sit and relax. I'll go up and place our orders."

He walked to the counter and returned to her after what seemed an awfully long wait, considering there were only a handful of diners in the restaurant. He slid into the booth beside her and they sat, looking at Polly's photos while they waited for their food. In retrospect, some of them were quite humorous and Polly laughed like she hadn't in ages.

The burgers were greasy, yet delicious, and Polly found herself enjoying every bite. She and Sammy sat, long after their plates had been cleared away, reminiscing about their shared history.

Finally, nature beckoned. "Excuse me, Sam. I believe I have to visit the powder room."

"Take your time. In fact, while you're doing that I think I'll pop into the little gift shop next door. I want to buy a post card."

"A memento of Hope Haven?" she said, surprised.

"A memento of a beautiful day."

After she'd finished up in the Ladies Room, Polly walked next door to the gift shop; a garishly painted building filled with tacky, overpriced merchandise. She took stock of the T-shirts, the wind socks, the assorted trinkets and baubles. It was the sort of cheap rubbish that people on vacation might buy as souvenirs. She grimaced. People who lacked good taste.

Sammy stood at the counter, paying for his post card. The pungent aroma of incense filled the air, making her dizzy. "Are you almost ready, Sam?"

"I'm completely ready. Shall we?"

Taking his arm, she walked from the store. Out on the sidewalk, he handed her a small cardboard jewelry box.

"What's this?"

"Just a little something I'd like you to have."

Puzzled, she opened the box. A brooch nestled in a square of gray Styrofoam. It was a hot air balloon, fake gold, sparkling with fake rubies. Its basket was painted silver and littered with rhinestones. It would go perfectly with her dollar store pearls. She snickered, and then her snicker built to a giggle. Before she knew it, she was laughing so hard she couldn't catch her breath.

"Sam, I'm sorry. That has got to be the gaudiest piece of jewelry I've ever laid eyes on."

"Here. Take a photo of it."

She complied, and then he removed it from its box and pinned it to her coat. "This will have to do, for now. This summer I'll take you up in a real one."

A wave of melancholy washed over her. I hope so, dear man, she thought. Oh, I do hope so.

"Ready to get back at it?" Sam asked.

"Sure."

They spent the next couple of hours working down their list. By the time the church bell chimed four, Polly was so chilled she couldn't feel her feet.

"I've had enough walking, how about you?" Sam asked.

"But we're almost done. We can't quit now," Polly protested through chattering teeth.

"We only have a couple of items left. We can easily find them at the lake. Let's head home."

In the car, Sam turned the heat to full power and Polly soaked it up, welcoming it with every chilled bone in her body. Before long she was feeling drowsy. As the car bumped up the winding road home, she felt her eyes begin to close. When she became aware of the lack of movement, she opened her eyes and saw that Sammy had driven to the Townline Bridge.

She gazed up at the gleaming silver structure that spread out like eagles' wings above the water. "I've always loved this bridge."

"Remember the summers we used to come down here as kids?"

She smiled. "Of course."

Her memory meandered back to her childhood, when she spent many summer evenings hunting for crawdads with the other neighborhood children along the river bank. Guided by a will of their own, her thoughts wandered to another evening, many years later. The evening Sam had taken her to a high school dance. Afterward they'd sat in his father's car beneath the bridge and talked for hours. It was the first time he'd ever kissed her.

Pulling the camera from her purse, she photographed the bridge through the windshield.

"Only one item left," Sam said. "Photograph an angel."

"I suppose we could drive over to St. Michael's. They have an angel statue beside the front entrance. Or maybe that's a cherub..."

Taking the camera from her hands, he snapped her photo.

"Now why did you do that?"

"You're my angel, Polly Church," he said softly.

Her eyes filled with tears. "I should be photographing you, you know. You're the angel, Sam. All of the kind, thoughtful things you do... Thank you. For today. For everything." Her voice dropped to a choked whisper. "I needed this."

His hand was warm as it covered hers.

"This is the first day in weeks I haven't dwelt on ... on what's going on inside me."

"The first of many, Polly."

"I don't know how long—"

He silenced her with the gentlest of kisses. "For however long we have left, my love. For however long we have left."

•

Polly arrived home at five o'clock to find Wendy sitting at the kitchen table, staring out the window. Given the girl's recent mood, she was surprised when she spoke to her.

"Hi, Aunt Polly."

She turned on a lamp. "Goodness, why are you sitting here in the dark?"

"I was watching the birds come to your feeder. I didn't realize it was getting dark. Where'd you go? I thought you'd be here when I got home."

Polly set the camera on the table, then shrugged out of her coat. "I had some errands to run in Hope Haven."

"What's the camera for?"

"I took a few photos. I was hoping you could help me print them out, later."

Wendy shrugged. "I guess." Turning the camera on, she scrolled through the photos. "What is all this?"

"If you must know, I've been on a photo scavenger hunt. It's great fun. The Internet provides you with a list, and you have to go around and photograph each item listed."

"Why is there a picture of you?"

"Because the list called for a diva. Don't you think your old aunt qualifies?"

Wendy smirked. "If you say so, Aunt Polly." She set the camera back on the table. "You must have had a blast today."

"Why do you say that?"

"Because. You're, like, glowing."

"Old women don't glow. Now why don't you get a head start on your homework while I make us some dinner?"

"I don't have any homework."

"Wonderful. Then you can set the table while I change my clothes."

In the bathroom, Polly shed her slacks and sweater and pulled on a cozy flannel lounging suit, all the while thinking back over the day. It was a day filled with memories she'd long treasure and she couldn't thank Sam enough for having planned it for her. She used the toilet and then washed her hands in the sink. Glancing in the mirror, she studied her reflection with surprise. Darned if she wasn't glowing.

Chapter Sixteen

Chase had studied it from every angle and considered every possible scenario. No detail had been overlooked. No matter which way it played out, he was ready for it. There was nothing left to do now but wait.

At six forty five on Friday evening he once again cruised past the Beacon Street address. He parked a block away, where he could see without being seen. He was only mildly surprised at the buzz of activity going on in front of the building. He considered the crowd of teenagers that had gathered; boys playing hackey sack and shoving each other while girls tottered in high heels, showing off for them. It looked as though Tito had done his job well. There must have been two dozen of them.

When the door opened and the teenagers started to disappear inside, he got out of his car and headed toward the building. He was almost to the front door when he a soft voice called out behind him.

"Hey."

He stared in disbelief as Lacy stepped out of the doorway of an abandoned building.

"What are you doing here?"

"The same thing as you, evidently. And by the way, you shouldn't lie. You're terrible at it."

He was busted and he knew it. This was the one scenario he hadn't planned for, but he could tell by the defiance in her eyes there'd be no getting her to wait in the car this time.

"So what's your plan, Sherlock?" he asked.

"I'm going inside."

"You're just going to walk in blind?"

She nodded toward the last of the teenagers disappearing inside the building. "They don't look all that threatening. I think I can handle myself."

"That's probably why he chose them."

Chase stepped ahead of her inside the hallway, fully expecting to be bounced back out the door. No one confronted him. From the dim hallway, he could hear a buzz of voices. He guided Lacy to the meeting room, and stopped cold. The tarps were folded neatly in a corner, and the center of the room was filled with folding chairs. Some outdated stereo equipment had been set up, and was playing some sort of snappy gospel music. Down in the front, two chairs sat beside a battered wooden podium, and from behind the podium, the big Latino waved at him. Chase waved back.

"What's going on?" Lacy whispered.

"I'm not sure. It might all be some sort of elaborate front."

"What should we do?"

"Let's sit down, see what happens."

They took their places among the teenagers. When the conversation died down, the big Latino spoke.

"I'm glad you all could make it down here tonight. I see some new faces. Welcome to Hope Haven Church of the Cross. Youth Pastor Dominick has a couple of announcements to make before we get started. I hope you'll come away from here tonight with a blessing, but I want to remind you, it's not just about the music. I hope to see you back here on Sunday morning at ten for our regular service. Pastor Dominick?"

A younger, smaller Latino man stepped up to the podium. He talked about something called Project Youth, and their upcoming missionary trip to Mexico. He announced that their loose change campaign had so far netted five hundred and seventy three dollars and the teens hooted. They turned sober again when he spoke of a missing neighborhood girl named Moniqua Rodriguez. Of how she'd gotten off the school bus a few days before and simply disappeared. "We can only guess what caused Moniqua to run away," he said somberly. "We can only guess at the trials that weighed upon her heart. But we have to trust that by God's grace, she'll find her way back home." He bowed his head and said a prayer for Moniqua, one for Project Youth, and then one more for that night's service. At last he unfolded his hands and said, "Now let's get our hearts and minds ready to worship God. Let's offer a round of applause for our music director, Brother De La Fuente."

A young Latino man stood and walked to the front of the building, carrying a guitar, and Chase sucked in a breath. He was the spitting image of Angel, only much younger, much less tainted looking. Lacy shot him a look of total disbelief as Tito sat down and began to play his guitar. His skill with the guitar and his soulful voice whipped the teens into a frenzy as he sang lively choruses about hope and peace and love. They stood in waves, hands clapping, arms waving in the air, like it was some sort of cosmic pep rally. Chase sat back, completely stunned. Then he cracked a smile. It was kind of funny, if you thought about it.

Tito sang and sang, and the more Chase thought about it, the funnier it became. A tremor of laughter escaped him, and he hid it behind a cough. Lacy nudged him, her eyes questioning, and then he lost it completely. With a loud guffaw, he stood and hurried outside.

She was right behind him. "What just happened in there?"

"I think—" He stopped to catch his breath, and a fresh wave of laughter struck. "I think Tito got religion."

"But I saw him in the neighborhood, bullying that boy."

"No, Lacy. You saw him talking to a boy. Nothing more. Don't you see? We both broke the cardinal rule of police investigation. We saw what we expected to see, instead of what was right there in front of us. I, of all people, should have known better."

"I guess now we know what he was doing in the old neighborhood. He was recruiting, all right. Recruiting members for his church."

Chase lost it again. "When Angel told me he was afraid Tito was getting into something he shouldn't be, I assumed he meant drugs, or even petty theft. This was the last damned thing I expected."

She cracked a smile, then giggled. "You wanna get out of here?"

"Yeah. I think this crowd's a little rowdy for me." They walked to his car and got in. "The thing is, I wouldn't mind coming back on Sunday. I'd still like to talk to him."

Her eyes gleamed. "Can I come with you this time, or do I have to take the bus again?"

"Your call, Sherlock."

"Pick me up at eight then. We'll have breakfast first." She giggled again, pulling him close. "Now shut up and kiss me."

Chapter Seventeen

Wendy ran her dust cloth over the coffee table, not bothering to move the vase and the set of coasters out of her way. She'd already done more than enough. She'd washed the dishes, vacuumed the floors, dusted the furniture and all of Aunt Polly's knickknacks. She was done. Dee-Oh-Enn-Ee. Just a couple more days and she'd be out of here.

It was three o'clock on Saturday afternoon and her mind was spinning with details. There was a lot to do in a day and a half and she was running out of time. Her head overflowed with lists of tasks to be completed before Monday came. Before she made her great escape. She'd have to play it smart, if she was going to get away with it.

Putting the cleaning supplies back in the closet, she went upstairs to her bedroom. Her glance swept across the cluttered space, taking in each of her possessions in turn. She'd have to leave most of them behind. She'd take only what would fit in her backpack. She went over her mental list: a pair of jeans, a couple extra shirts, her sketchpad and pencils, a toothbrush. Her gaze rested on her jewelry box. She'd take her ear gauges and her studs, and the bracelet Ms. Denning had bought for her last Halloween. The rest of it would just be a burden. And she didn't need unnecessary burdens. She'd have to travel light.

She sat down on her bed with a sigh. It was taking everything she had to act normal around Aunt Polly. She had to admit, it hurt her, seeing her aunt so happy. Because she knew the reason behind Polly's renewed cheerfulness. She was planning to shove Wendy off on Dove Denning. Aunt Polly saw her as a burden. A cross she no longer wanted to bear. Ms. Denning must have told Polly she'd take up the cross, like that dude in the Bible who carried Jesus' cross up the hill. Ms. Denning was a modern-day Good Samaritan. But Wendy had no intention of going where she wasn't wanted.

She went over her plan again in her mind. On Monday morning she'd get on the school bus. Once she reached the high school, she'd have to find a way to sneak off without being noticed. That would be the tricky part. Then she'd walk the five blocks to the bus station. She'd look at all of the schedules and go as far away as the forty dollars in her pocket would take her. It didn't really matter where she went. Probably no one would bother to look for her anyway.

•

The campground was almost ready for Emma's winter carnival. Chase wouldn't have thought it possible, given the short amount of time they'd had to pull it all together. On Saturday afternoon, Shane assigned him the task of finishing up Santa's Palace, so after lunch, he gathered up a dozen posts, along with the life-sized reindeer and the giant candy canes, and drove down to the gazebo.

He nailed the decorations to the posts and then set about pounding them into the ground. He was finally getting into the rhythm of it when his mallet slipped and crashed down on his thumb. Pain shrieked along the nerve endings in his hand and he cursed. Throwing the mallet, he studied the dark shadow beneath his nail. He was no kind of handyman, that was for sure. But it didn't really matter. In a couple of months he'd be out of here.

Retrieving the mallet from a nearby snow bank, he started again. He pounded the rest of the posts into the ground and stowed the mallet in his tool belt. It wasn't that he minded working at the campground. Shane and Emma had been decent to him. And besides that, it gave him something to occupy his time while he was waiting for his three-month leave of absence to be up. There were worse jobs than stringing Christmas lights and driving nails. He could probably even get good at it, given enough time. But in his heart, he'd never be anything but a cop.

His thoughts wandered back to the night before and the strange turn of events with Tito De la Fuente. He'd have to sharpen up, re-hone his investigative instincts. A picture of Tito playing his guitar for the joyful crowd of teens popped into his head and he smiled. Despite the fact that he'd been wrong about Tito's activities, he was glad it had played out the way it did.

A small shadow crossed his heart. He still had another matter to settle with Tito, and he wasn't looking forward to it. And now that he knew about Lacy's dream of owning her own bakery, he'd have to see what he could do to help that dream along. With those tasks completed, he'd be free of his guilt. Free to return to his real life.

Before he could stop them, a parade of pictures marched through his consciousness; pictures of Lacy, her eyes shining as she wielded an air hockey paddle, Lacy, preparing his dinner in her kitchen, holding him, kissing him. His lovely Lacy. God, how he loved her.

The thought came unbidden, and he pushed it from his mind. He'd never meant for it to go this far. He had no business falling in love with Lacy Kennedy. Or with anyone else. Even if she agreed to pull up her roots and follow him to New York, which he could never in good conscience ask her to do, it would never work out. When it came to women, his track record over the last few years had been dismal, at best. His long, unpredictable work hours made maintaining a relationship an impossibility. It was going to hurt like hell, but there was no way around it. He'd have to let her go, and the sooner he did it, the better.

Chapter Eighteen

After a sleepless night Chase rose from his bed, showered and shaved, and appeared in the kitchen wearing a pair of navy blue slacks and a blue button down shirt. Maxine's glance swept over him. "Where are you off to this morning, all dressed up?"

"Believe it or not, I'm going to church."

Her eyes betrayed surprise, but she simply nodded, as if it were the most natural thing in the world.

Driving to Lacy's apartment, his hands gripped the wheel. Could he go through with all he had planned? There was still time to back out. Maybe he'd text her and tell her he had the flu.

He pulled into a spot out front and sat for long moments, trying to decide. And then the front door opened and she appeared, and there was no more time. His gaze took in her black slacks and the cream colored blouse that peeked from beneath her jacket. A pair of silver clips held her hair in check, but a few strands escaped and curled softly at her temples. *Lord, Lord, Lord.* She opened the door and climbed inside. "Good morning."

"Morning."

"Do I look okay? I don't have a lot of what you'd call church clothes. I feel like I look like a cocktail waitress."

"You look gorgeous. And anyway, I don't think this is a real dressy kind of church."

They drove into Hope Haven and Lacy suggested they eat at a cafe called Boomer's. He ordered a stack of hotcakes but was unable to eat more than a few bites. His upcoming conversation with Tito was weighing heavily on his mind. When they'd finished their breakfast, he threw a handful of bills on the table and stood. "Ready?"

"Wow, Chase, lighten up."

"What do you mean?"

"You should see your face. You look like you're heading to an execution, not a church service."

"I guess I'm feeling a little bit apprehensive."

"About Tito?"

"Yeah."

"It'll be okay." Her hand crept into his, so soft and warm and reassuring that he almost believed it would be.

As they walked into the white building on Beacon Street, his stomach lurched and he once again reached for her hand. He held it fast as they slid into folding chairs in the back. The room was nearly full, and he glanced at the collection of faces around him; men and women, children and teenagers. Some of them black, some white. Most of them Latino. After several moments of happy chatter, the big man stepped up to the podium.

"Good morning, brothers and sisters," he said in his big, raspy voice.

"Good morning, Pastor Torres."

The big man's eyes swept over his congregation. They rested on Chase, and he smiled. "It's real good to see you all here this morning. Let's take some time and ask God's blessing on this service. Let's take some time to remember Moniqua Rodriguez, and to believe in God for her safe return."

After a short, powerful prayer, the pastor sat down and Tito appeared with his guitar. As he sang, his large, doe eyes scanned every face. When he spied Lacy's, his face lit up in a smile. He sang a few more hymns, the congregation singing along. When the music was finished, the big man once again took the podium.

"This is a season of blessings, a season of gifts. In this season of thankfulness, God wants you to know he's prepared gifts for each and every one of you."

Chase had intended to sit back, to tune him out, but his words and his voice were so compelling he found he couldn't stop listening. He sat, riveted to the big man's stories, stories he'd heard long ago in Sunday school. He talked about the woman's gift of precious oil to a weary Christ, contrasted it with the story of the prodigal son, and how he'd squandered his father's gifts on prostitutes and booze. Today, sitting in that cinder block room, what seemed a lifetime later, the stories seemed so much more relevant. Before Chase knew it, the hour had passed.

"Brothers and sisters," the big man said, "Let us not squander God's gifts. Let's not squander one precious moment of the gift of life! Wherever you are today, God wants you to know that He has gifts He's ready, willing, and able to give you. Gifts of love, joy, and peace. If you're in a bad place today, God wants you to know that you don't have to stay there. He's ready, willing and able to carry your burdens. What's burdening you today? What's robbing you of joy and peace? God invites you to come now and lay down your burdens on His altar. What would you have God do for you today, brothers and sisters? What gift would you like to receive from God? You don't have to do more than come and ask. For our Lord has told us, whatsoever you ask in my name, you will receive."

The atmosphere in the room felt super-charged. Tito strummed his guitar. People got up from their chairs and headed toward the podium. Chase felt the pressure building again, the pressure of the burdens he'd carried his entire life. Burdens of resentment and bitterness, of guilt and shame. He couldn't stand up, couldn't join the flow of people streaming toward the altar. He wasn't a demonstrative man. He felt a sense of expectancy in the room, and then he felt Lacy's hand slide into his, and he felt like anything was possible. And though he wasn't a spiritual man, and though he was woefully out of practice, he bowed his head, and he prayed.

When the service was over, they stood. Lacy's expression echoed the sense of peace that filled him from head to toe. And then, suddenly, Tito was there.

"Lacy?" He reached for her, hugged her close. "It's so good to see you, girl."

"Hi, Tito. It's great to see you, too."

"Wow, it's been awhile, huh? You look great." His glance moved over her, and then moved to Chase. "Is this your boyfriend?"

Lacy hesitated and Chase blurted, "Yeah, I am. Chase Alexander. Nice to meet you."

"Good to meet you, Chase." They exchanged a handshake. Tito's skin was smooth, his hands, almost delicate. The hands of a music man.

"I haven't seen you around the Cove in a long time," Lacy said.

"I've been staying with the Pastor and his wife."

"I hope you don't mind me asking, Tito. But how did you get into this?"

He smiled. "Two months ago I would have told you it was all a coincidence, but I now I know there are no accidents with God." He told them the story, then, of how he'd been hanging out on the street corner on that warm September night, playing his guitar, hoping to make a few extra bucks. A great big dude with a cross tattooed on his neck happened by. He'd thrown a twenty-dollar bill into Tito's open guitar case, along with the address of his church. He'd invited Tito to come down that Sunday, had told him God could use him.

"So the next Sunday I took the bus down to Hope Haven." He grinned. "I was hoping to get some more money. But in the end I got something so much more valuable. I started putting together the music for Pastor's church services, and eventually he asked me to be the music director. I started working with the youth group part time. I wanted to try and help these kids, the way I wish someone would have helped me. And then after what happened to Angel, I chucked it all and jumped in with both feet."

"I heard about that," Lacy said softly. "I'm so sorry, Tito."

Chase felt his insides tighten.

"I talked to him a few weeks ago," Tito said, his hand sweeping the room. "I told him about this. I told him everything we'd looked for all our lives, I'd found it, right here. Angel, he couldn't trust it. He wanted me to get out of it.

"I knew he was back into selling drugs. Every time he called, I could hear in his voice that he was high. I begged him to come home, to come clean, before something bad happened. Then a few weeks ago I got another call, from the Queens Police. They told me my brother had been shot by an undercover cop. They wanted to mail me his things." Tears gathered in his eyes. "There was nothing in his wallet but two pictures, Lacy. One of you, and one of me." He took a moment to compose himself, then said softly, "He made some bad mistakes, Angel. But no matter what else he was, he was my brother."

Lacy squeezed Chase's hand. His heart pounded, because the moment he'd been waiting for had come. "This cop," he said. "What would you say to him if he was standing in front of you. Right here. Right now?"

Tito looked him square in the eye. An understanding passed between them, and in that moment, Chase saw that he knew.

"I'd say I forgive you, brother."

The statement was made with sincerity and it went straight to Chase's soul. The tears he'd been unable to shed since the night he lost his mother burned in his eyes. They spilled over and ran down his face in rivers. And with each one that fell, he felt a lifting of the hatred and resentment he'd carried for twenty-four years.

•

In the car, Lacy pulled out the clips and let her hair fall free, "Wow. That was intense."

"Yeah."

"I'm glad you talked to him."

"Me, too." He started the car and pulled out into the street. "I feel like I can move ahead now. Like when I go back, I'll be a better cop."

She glanced at him in surprise. "I thought you weren't a cop any more."

"That's just temporary. I'm going back to Queens."

She stared at him, feeling as if she'd been slapped. "You are?"

"It's just a three-month leave of absence, Lacy. I thought I told you that."

"No, you didn't."

She fell quiet, not trusting herself to speak. When they reached her apartment house, he turned off the engine and reached for the door handle.

"You can't come up today. I have things to do," she blurted. "I got hired to make a wedding cake. I have to get started on it."

"Okay, no problem. Want to go to a movie later?"

"I'm going to be busy all day."

"Alright. Can I call you tomorrow?"

She forced a smile. "Sure."

She held it in until the door to her apartment closed behind her, then let her tears fall, her earlier feelings of peace and goodwill suddenly evaporated. The big man's words echoed in her head, taunting her. Words about grace and faith, about God's love and His lavish gifts. She should have known it was too good to be true. She'd only asked God for one small gift. Obviously He'd said no.

Chapter Nineteen

Early Monday morning, the sound of Wendy's name pulled her from a fitful sleep, a sleep which seemed to have come only moments before. She'd drifted in and out of consciousness the whole night, her feverish mind racing with plans, refusing to shut down.

"Wendy, dear. It's time to get up."

She opened her eyes to weak daylight filtering through the window and Aunt Polly's face hovering above her own. She looked at the clock on her nightstand and tried to focus on the glowing numbers it displayed.

"What time is it?"

"It's a little before seven."

The words registered and she bolted upright. "Why did you let me sleep so late? I'm going to miss the bus!"

"Relax," Polly said calmly. "It seems there's some sort of problem with a water main at your school. Classes have been delayed by two hours. Your bus won't arrive until after nine."

"Oh."

"I'll be leaving shortly for an appointment in the city, so I thought I'd better get you up and moving before I go."

It took Wendy's sleep-starved brain a moment to process the information. The bus was going to be late. Her plan would be delayed by more than two hours. Damn.

Pulling on yesterday's sweat pants and tee shirt, she made her way downstairs to the kitchen. Aunt Polly set a fresh cup of coffee at her place at the table. "Would you like a couple of slices of toast?"

Her stomach clenched. "No thanks."

The morning paper sat folded on the table. Wendy opened it up. A headline screamed at her from the front page: Three Teens

Arrested In Shadow Lake Burglary.

All of her blood seemed to rush to her head. It roared in her ears as she scanned through the story. Three Sunset Cove teens had been apprehended the night before while attempting to burglarize a home in Cardinal Bay. They were taken to the police station, and after lengthy questioning, confessed to their involvement in the month-long rash of burglaries in the Shadow Lake community. Eighteen-year-old Cassidy Hubbard had been placed under arrest, along with two juvenile offenders whose names were being withheld.

Wendy sat staring at the words, feeling numb, wondering why Cassidy had confessed. No way could her friend be involved in the robberies. In fact, on the night Aunt Polly's house had been burglarized, Cass had been with Wendy. As she thought back to the night they'd gone to hear Noise Pollution practice, a cold realization dawned. Cassidy had known nobody would be home that night, Wendy had told her all about Aunt Polly's Sialia meeting. She'd told Cassidy a lot of things, like how mortified she was that their math teacher, Mr. Holmes, was a member of Aunt Polly's Bluebird Society, how he always mentioned it during class. She'd handed Cass and her low-life friends a perfect opportunity to burglarize Mr. Holmes' house. She'd thought Cass was her friend. How could she have been such a fool?

A car horn sounded out front, startling her.

"That will be Mr. Delaney, here to take me to my appointment," Aunt Polly said, pulling on her coat and gloves. "I'll see you later this afternoon."

"All right, Aunt Polly."

"Have a nice day."

After Polly left, Wendy sipped her coffee, rereading the newspaper article. Mick had been right about her friends all along. She could just picture his face this morning, as he read the article, could almost hear his smug I told you so. A horrible thought occurred. Mick probably assumed she was involved in the burglaries. The thought caused both pain and anger. Who cared what Mick Lucy thought? The sooner she got out of here the better.

She set the paper aside, going over the details again in her mind. She'd wear three layers of clothes. With the extra pair of jeans and hoodie she'd stowed in her backpack that would give her a total of four outfits to start her new life with. She'd also smuggled a jar of peanut butter and a box of granola bars out of Aunt Polly's cupboards. Hopefully after she paid for her bus ticket she'd have enough cash left over to eat for a day or two.

Once she got to wherever she was going, she'd find a homeless shelter to stay in. That would put a roof over her head until she found some sort of job. She bit her lip. That was the part that worried her. Everyone knew that jobs were really hard to find right now. Hopefully there'd be a diner where she could wait on tables. Heck, she'd even wash dishes.

She poured another cup of coffee and moved to the living room. She sat in front of the oversized window, where she could watch the birds that came to feed at Aunt Polly's feeder. Thanks to Polly, she knew most of their names. She recognized a pair of chickadees; lively, chirpy little birds wearing shiny black berets. A nuthatch, all dressed in blue and gray, crept along the tree trunk, waiting for his chance at the feeder. She also noted some juncos and some finches. Best of all were the pair of cardinals.

Of all the birds that came to their little feeder, Wendy loved the cardinals best. She loved the bold, beautiful males, who livened up the winter landscape with their coats of fiery red. She loved the way they ruled the bird feeder, not taking anyone's crap. She even loved the females, with their soft brown feathers and the blush of pink on their under parts. Even more so, since Polly had told her that the cardinal was one of but a handful of female birds who possessed the gift of song. After Aunt Polly told her that, she'd learned to listen for it, to identify the lady cardinal's soft, melodious warble. *Whoit, whoit, whoit. What-cheer, what-cheer, what-cheer.*

She noticed the birds bickering, flitting at one another, fighting over the seed. The feeder was getting low. She'd take the time to fill it before she left. The thought caused a nervous fluttering sensation in her tummy and she took a breath to steel her nerves. She couldn't start having second thoughts now. Not when Aunt Polly seemed so happy. She frowned, thinking of all of the doctor appointments Polly seemed to be going to lately. Heck, maybe that was just a lame excuse. Aunt Polly and Mr. Delaney could be out picking engagement rings, for all she knew, eagerly awaiting the day Wendy was gone and out of their way.

"Today's the day," she murmured.

A dark shadow fell across the feeder and Wendy's gaze was drawn back to the window, where a red shouldered hawk circled in the sky above the yard. The hawks were feisty, mouthy birds and Wendy hated them. Aunt Polly had told her again and again that it was not for the sake of cruelty, when the hawks dove at squirrels, rabbits and small birds, their sharp talons extended, ready to seize. She said it was just a part of the circle of life. And Wendy knew that, on some level. But she hated the way the hawks terrorized the song birds that came to the feeder. She knew all about how it felt to be bullied.

The shadow deepened and Wendy watched, horrified, as the hawk swooped down at the feeder, scattering the juncos and the finches. The hawk made a bee line for the female cardinal and a scream stuck in Wendy's throat. The male cardinal burst into action, darting toward the hawk, and then away again, the air filled with his sharp cry of anger. Momentarily thrown off guard, the hawk missed his target and flew away, but in the chaos, the female cardinal panicked and flitted toward the house, bashing headfirst into the picture window.

"Oh, God." Pulling on a hoodie, Wendy rushed outside. The cardinal lay in the snow beneath the window, silent and bloodied. Dropping to her knees, Wendy lifted the bird gently in her hands, being extra careful to keep its wings close to its body in case it panicked again.

"You'll be alright," she whispered, hoping beyond hope it was true.

The male cardinal shrieked at her from the treetops as, tears streaming from her eyes, she carried his broken lady inside.

In the back room, she set the cardinal in a laundry basket on a soft towel, and then hurried to the basement, where she knew Aunt Polly kept several bird cages.

She selected a medium-sized cage and carried it back upstairs to the kitchen. She remembered Polly once telling her about an abandoned bluebird fledgling she'd rescued, and how she'd fashioned a light bulb above the tiny nest of cotton batting she'd made, to keep the baby warm. Thinking of how cold the cardinal's body had felt, she retrieved a rice pack from the cupboard, put it in the microwave, and set it for a minute and a half. When the timer rang, she removed the rice pack, punched a hollow in the center with her fist, and set it inside the cage. Carefully, barely daring to breathe, she laid the cardinal in its center. Aunt Polly had also told her that stress can do more harm to an injured bird than its actual wounds, but still, she couldn't resist softly stroking the bird's feathers, whispering words of encouragement.

"Please. Oh, please be okay."

The bird lay, still and silent, its eyes closed and Wendy wept for the sorrow of it all. For the sacrificial love of the male cardinal, and the female's needless, reckless flight. She'd been safe, perfectly safe the whole entire time. And she hadn't even know it.

•

It had been a busy morning. Maxine's car was in the shop, so Chase had spent the morning running her around. He'd taken her to the grocery store, and to a doctor's appointment. He'd waited in line at the pharmacy, his impatience flaring, as a woman purchased handfuls of lottery tickets, scratched them off at the counter, and purchased more. It was one of his biggest pet peeves. Why, oh why couldn't they designate a separate line for these lottery fanatics?

After he'd taken Maxine home and settled her into a chair with a cup of her favorite green tea, he called Shane and told him he'd be in at noon. There was one more thing he still had to do.

At eleven o'clock he drove to the empty building on Arbor Street. A burgundy Impala was parked out front. He pulled to the curb behind it and a woman got out. She was blonde and petite, tanned like some sort of Mexican sun goddess, dressed to the nines. "Are you Chase?" she asked.

"That's me."

She smiled. "I'm Mary Nevinger. It's nice to meet you." She extended a small, pink-tipped hand and he shook it politely.

He followed her to the front entrance and waited while she fitted a key into the lock box.

"I have to tell you, you picked a great time to buy. The owner is very anxious."

Of that, Chase had no doubt. His glance took in the peeling paint and the warped door casing.

She pushed open the door. Its hinges screamed in protest. "In fact, if we play our cards right, we could close in as early as three days."

Inside, the building had a sour, neglected smell about it. Chase scrutinized the large, open room. A chipped Formica-topped counter ran the length of the right hand side, with several mismatched tables and chairs scattered in the space to the left. A dropped ceiling sagged precariously above his head. Beneath his feet, the tile was dirty and broken.

"As I said on the phone, it will need some cosmetics, but the building is structurally sound," Mary Nevinger said brightly. "For the price, you really can't go wrong."

He followed her to the back of the building, into a large kitchen area with two oversized ovens and gaping holes that God-knew-what kind of equipment had once filled.

"How's the wiring?" he asked.

"There's a fuse box out back."

Finding the box, he opened it. A tangle of wires and blackened fuses stared him in the face. He quickly shut the door. "Looks like the whole building will have to be rewired. That won't be cheap."

Mary Nevinger's smile slipped. "No, I suppose it won't."

A back staircase led up to a one-bedroom apartment. Like the rooms downstairs, it was dingy and badly in need of paint. But Chase could see possibilities in the exposed brick walls and the oversized window that let in plenty of natural light.

A separate entrance from the street led to a large room with a private half bath. As Lacy had said, the space would be perfect for an office. His gaze traveled upward, to where a brown stain crept across the ceiling. "Does the roof leak?"

The realtor smiled, ready with an answer. "It did at one time, but it's recently been re-shingled and sealed. So ... what do you think?"

"What did you say the seller's asking price was?"

"Thirty-two thousand dollars."

"Tell him I'll give him twenty. And not a penny more."

•

The school bus came and went, and still Wendy sat with the female cardinal. She couldn't leave home now. Couldn't even think of it. Not when she held the fate of the little bird in her hands.

Throughout the long morning she sat by the cage in the back room, willing the bird to stand up, to be all right. But it lay on its rice pack, still and quiet and seemingly indifferent to her concern.

It was early afternoon before it occurred to her that Aunt Polly must have books. She was a certified wildlife rehabilitation specialist, which meant she must have stacks and stacks of books on the subject. Why hadn't Wendy thought of it sooner?

Hurrying upstairs, she hesitated outside the door to Aunt Polly's bedroom. It was a forbidden zone. The only area of the house in which she wasn't allowed. Bracing herself, she pushed open the door.

Aunt Polly's bedroom was a cozy little nest of framed photographs and handmade pottery. A colorful quilt lay across a double bed, which was strewn with pillows. Hurrying past, Wendy made her way to the little room out back, a sun porch that Polly had insulated and made over into an office. An antique roll top desk held a laptop and a neat stack of papers. Above the desk, the degree in horticulture Aunt Polly had earned at the university after Uncle Benny's death sat proudly in the center of the wall, framed in glossy black and matted in a soft, mossy green color. Wendy took a moment to admire the photos of birds, deer, and even a black bear Aunt Polly had taken. On an opposite wall, a large window offered a sweeping view of Shadow Lake. The space was lovely and serene and Wendy could see why Polly had chosen it for her office.

A floor-to-ceiling book case took up the opposite wall. Wendy walked over to the books and scanned their titles until she found one that looked promising. Opening its cover, she sat down at Aunt Polly's desk and flipped through its pages. When she found a chapter titled *First Aid for Birds,* she smiled.

"Yes!"

Back downstairs, she carefully removed the cardinal from its cage and examined her. There didn't seem to be any damage other than the blood that encrusted her face. The book said to apply Monsel's salts to the wounds, and Wendy had rooted through Aunt Polly's various concoctions until she'd found it.

Using a soapy cotton ball, she cleaned the wound, and then, reading the directions carefully, she applied the Monsel's salts. She placed a small square of gauze over the wound, applying gentle pressure, all the while speaking softly to bird. It struggled weakly in her hands, which Wendy took as a good sign.

With the bleeding stopped and the wound thoroughly cleaned, Wendy could see that the bird had suffered only a minor cut at the side of her bill. Referring again to the book, she prepared a mixture of sugar and water, dipped her fingertip into it, and lightly rubbed it on the side of the bird's bill, taking extra care not to get water into its naves. To her delight, the bird's bill opened to receive her sugary gift, and Wendy offered more. Seeing the rice pack had cooled, she warmed it again in the microwave and set it back in the cage. She'd just returned the book to Aunt Polly's office when she heard the front door open downstairs.

She crept down the staircase to see Aunt Polly standing in the foyer, a frown of disapproval on her face.

"It's only a little past two," she said. "How come you're not at school?"

The old woman's displeasure was more than Wendy could bear, and her words came out in a rush. "I was going to get ready to go. Right after you left. But a hawk came to the feeder. A red shouldered hawk. It swooped down and all the birds scattered, except this one male cardinal. He tried to save his mate, but she got scared and flew toward the house. She hit the window and was lying in the snow. I got a cage from the cellar and put her in it. Then I remembered about the heat, so I warmed up a rice pack for her. I cleaned her up the best I could. Then I tried giving her sugar water. She drank a little, but I don't know if she'll be okay. It was awful." The words caught in her throat and became a sob.

"Well then," Aunt Polly said, her tone softening. "Let's have a look at this cardinal of yours."

Wendy led her aunt to the back room and quietly opened the door. To her amazement, the cardinal stood on her feet, making soft chirping noises.

"Oh, she's a beauty, for certain." Polly smiled. "It looks like whatever you've done has been a success. Now tell me again, more slowly, how it happened."

Wendy repeated the story, filling in the details this time. When she'd finished, Polly looked at her in amazement. "How did you know what to do?"

Wendy looked away from her. "I saw it in one of your books."

"I see. So you went into my private office?"

"I'm sorry, Aunt Polly. I was so scared for her. I didn't know what else to do."

Without answering, Polly removed the bird from its cage and

inspected its bill. "She appears to be all right now. She probably has a slight concussion. I'm sure she'll be just fine in a few hours."

"Do you really think so?"

"I do. But we'll keep her overnight, just to be sure. Then we'll release her in the morning." She smiled. "I'm sure her poor husband is worried sick about her."

Wendy grinned.

"I'm proud of you, Wendy."

A sob escaped Wendy's lips. Despite her resolve not to cry, tears poured down her face. It felt good to hear those words, and she so desperately wanted to believe them.

Polly lifted a hand and awkwardly patted her shoulder. "I know it can be a disconcerting experience, caring for an injured bird. And you can't always save them. But you did a fine job. I'll make a wildlife rehabber out of you yet."

Wendy could hear her heartbeat roaring in her ears. She was afraid to ask, but more afraid not to know. "Does that mean you're not shipping me out?"

"Shipping you out, Wendy? What on earth would make you think that?"

Her gaze dropped to the floor. "I heard you on the phone with Ms. Denning. Talking about making arrangements for me."

"Oh, dear." Polly sighed.

"It's true, then?"

Polly sighed again. "I have something to tell you, child. Something I should have told you a long time ago. Come out to the kitchen. I feel in need of a cup of tea."

Later, over a soothing blend of herbal tea served in delicate rose-sprinkled tea cups, Polly told her about the cancer.

"So you see, that's why Ms. Denning called. Among her other gifts, she's what you call a medical empath. She dreamed about the cancer. Naturally, she was worried about what might happen to you. She's offered to raise you herself, and I think that would be wise. She can give you all of the things a young girl craves. She can give you a much more normal life than you'd have, living with a sick old woman."

"I don't want to have a normal life." Wendy heard herself say it and knew it to be the truth. Like the little cardinal, she'd been panicked, ready to take off in blind, reckless flight. When all the while she'd been perfectly safe. "I want to stay here with you, Aunt Polly. For as long as I possibly can."

"Oh, child. Are you sure?"

"I am sure, Aunt Polly. I know I've been a pain in the butt. But I'm going to change. I'm going to be better, now. I swear it."

With a tearful smile, Polly folded Wendy into her arms, and Wendy snuggled into the profound, lavender-scented love of her aunt's embrace, and held on for dear life.

Chapter Twenty

The last days before the winter carnival passed in frenzied activity at Shadow Lake campground. The kitchen was alive with laughter as the neighborhood women helped Emma frost her gingerbread cookies. Outside, there were vendor's booths to set up and string with holly boughs, and last minute decorating to be done in the rec hall. On Friday evening Emma, Shane and Chase took a last walk through the campground, double checking that all was in order. Since he'd played hockey in high school and was decidedly the best skater of the three, Shane put Chase in charge of the ice skating rink.

On Saturday morning Chase showed up at seven AM to find the campground already buzzing with excitement. In the rec hall, Noise Pollution was setting up their equipment and doing sound checks. In the house, Emma and Polly Church mixed up enormous batches of sweet mulled cider and eggnog. Gazing down the path, he saw that Shane and Mick had already lit the trails. The woods were luminous with thousands of feet of shimmering lights.

By ten o'clock the campground was a chaotic festival of activity. Sleigh bells twinkled merrily as the two sturdy old Clydesdales Emma had rented made their plodding way up and down the trails, laden with an antique sleigh and its riders. Children's shrieks of laughter were punctuated by the jolly *Ho Ho Ho* of the carnival Santa. Music boomed from the direction of the rec hall, where the band belted out their renditions of popular holiday classics. The scents of sugar waffles and Italian sausage hung in the air, making his mouth water. Everywhere he looked, there were people enjoying themselves.

He spent the day helping kids lace up their skates, monitoring the rink, and giving basic skating lessons to a few reluctant parents. All the while, his eyes scanned the crowd for a glimpse of Lacy's raven hair, her fawn colored jacket. He'd been crazy busy at the campground all week, working from early morning until late at night. He and Lacy hadn't done more than exchange a few hurried phone calls. When he'd called last night and reminded her about the carnival, she said she had other plans. He hoped beyond hope that she'd change her mind.

Especially now that he'd changed his.

Last Sunday, telling her straight out about his plans to return to Queens had seemed like the right thing to do. Why lead her on, when he was leaving in just a few more weeks? But being without her this week, he'd realized how much she meant to him. How empty his life was before she came into it. Touring the abandoned bakery, an idea had formed in his mind, like a window being thrown open wide. Going ahead with it would change his life, and that scared the hell out of him. Remembering the peace he'd felt in the little church on Beacon Street, he'd prayed for the second time in his life, asking God if it was the right thing to do. So far, he hadn't gotten an answer.

It was early evening, and most of the parents had dragged their reluctant children from the rink when she finally arrived. Chase was just considering locking the gates for the night when he saw her, a thin, jeans-clad figure in a flamboyant red ski cap, heading his way.

He smiled. "Well, look who's here. Plans fall through?"

"You could say that." Her glance swept across the empty rink. "Am I too late?"

"Nope."

"Where is everyone?"

"Most of the little ones have already left. The adults are probably down at the rec hall, listening to the music. But I'm still here."

She pulled two crumpled one-dollar bills from the pocket of her jeans. "In that case, I'd like a pair of skates, please. Size six."

He moved into the booth, found the appropriate size, and handed them to her with a flourish. As she sat down on a bench and laced them, a stray tendril of hair escaped her cap and fell across her face, looking so soft and silky that he ached to touch it.

Her skates laced, she stood and held out her hand. "Care to

dance?"

They linked arms and began to move together across the ice. He'd been skating all day, but this time it was different. Beside Lacy, under the twinkling lights with the music playing soft and faraway and her perfume filling his senses, the evening seemed suddenly enchanted. He didn't want to speak or even breathe as they skated around and around in their private wonderland. He didn't want to chance breaking the magical spell.

Finally, Lacy spoke. "So. Would you say this qualifies as having fun?"

He laughed softly. "I didn't say you don't know how to have fun, Lacy. And anyway, you've already proven you do."

"But would you say this qualifies, just hypothetically?"

"Just hypothetically, I ought to dump your cute little butt right in the snow bank."

"Just you try it, Mister."

He smiled. He did love a challenge. Scooping her up in his arms, he skated toward the edge of the rink, Lacy shrieking.

"If you do, I swear, you'll be sorry."

"Ooh. A tough guy."

"Chase, I mean it!"

Laughing, he set her down on the ice. "Okay, tough guy. You win. This time."

"Smart move. Now let me catch my breath." She bent over with her hands on her knees and pulled in a deep breath. Before he could react, she reached beside her and scooped up a handful of snow. Forming a perfect snowball, she threw it at him, hitting him square in the face. "Yeah! Now that's what I'm talkin' about!" She skated off, the deep, throaty laughter he loved trailing in the air behind her.

In the next moments an all out snowball war ensued. They took turns flinging powdery ammunition at each other until they were both breathless with laughter. "Okay, enough already!" Lacy said, gasping for air. "I'm freezing."

He drew up next to her. "Let me warm you, then." He pulled her close. "Better?"

She tilted her face to his. "Almost."

It was a clear invitation and he took full advantage of it. His lips came down on hers and he felt like his entire body was on fire as she returned his kiss.

All too soon, she ended it. "What you said to Tito on Sunday, about being my boyfriend?" she whispered. "I liked it."

Caught off guard, he could only stare at her. "What?"

"I liked the sound of it. Just thought I'd throw it out there."

Pushing away from him, she sped off across the rink. He followed, feeling strangely buoyant. God had given him his answer.

•

It had been a wonderful day.

When Sammy first proposed she don a red dress and be his Mrs. Santa, Polly's initial reaction was to refuse. It would be noisy, she told him. Crowded. Cold. But then he'd pointed out that number sixty-four on her seventy list was spend a day pretending to be someone else and she'd had no choice, really, except to go along with it. She was so glad now that she did. She'd spent the day surrounded by happy children. She'd listened to wish lists and handed out candy canes. She'd had her picture taken at least a hundred times. She'd received dozens of sticky kisses. And she'd never enjoyed a day more. But enough was enough. It was getting late now, and she was tired.

"I think most of the little ones have gone home," Sam said. "Shall we close up shop?"

"Oh, let's," she said gratefully. "I'm exhausted. And cold."

"Why don't we stop by the food tent for a cup of mulled cider to warm us up? After that I'm hoping I can talk you into taking a moonlit sleigh ride with me."

"You won't have to twist my arm too hard on that score," she told him. "Remember, take a horse-drawn carriage ride is one of the items on my seventy list."

Her gaze traveled across the gazebo to where Wendy was boxing up the last of the candy canes. She'd spent the day helping out in Santa's Palace and had even agreed to dress up like an elf without too much coercion.

"Wendy was a big help to us today, wasn't she?"

"She was invaluable. And the children really seem to love her."

"I think she enjoyed herself."

He smiled. "I know I did."

"Wendy," Polly called. "You've worked hard today. After you've finished putting up the candy, you can close up for the night. The rest of the evening is yours to do as you please."

"Okay, Aunt Polly."

After they'd enjoyed gingerbread cookies and tall mugs of warm cider, Polly and Sam made their way across the campground to where the carriage waited. A young man in a black velvet jacket and a top hat smiled in greeting.

"Care for a ride tonight?"

"Yes, please," Sam said. After handing the man a ten-dollar bill, he helped Polly up into the carriage. With a jerk of the reins and a tinkle of sleigh bells, they headed off down the path.

Polly's gaze swept over the snow-brushed evergreens, the twinkling lights. "My, isn't this lovely," she murmured.

Sammy's gloved hand covered hers. They rode in silence for awhile, and then Polly said, "I've spoken with Dove Denning. She said she'd be willing to help out with Wendy. When the time comes."

Sammy patted her hand. "That won't be for a long, long time."

She'd meant to tell him later, at home, in private. Certainly not in the presence of a stranger. But the carriage driver sat, ear buds in place, his head bobbing up and down to his own private soundtrack. On this wondrous, moon swept evening, the timing seemed perfect, and so she blurted, "I'm having the treatments, Sam. I'm going to go ahead with it."

With a tender smile, he folded her into his embrace. "That's the very best Christmas gift you could have given me, Polly."

"There is one more," she said, thinking of the lovely book of bird illustrations she'd bought for him in the city. "But you'll have to wait for Christmas Day."

"Which reminds me." He pulled an envelope from the pocket of his coat. "I thought about saving this for Christmas Day, but I think I'd rather give it to you now."

"Really, Sam. You're worse than a child," she scolded. But she couldn't help the flush of pleasure that crept across her face. Removing her gloves, she opened the envelope and pulled out two bisque-colored tickets. She squinted at the calligraphy script.

"Oh, Sam. This is too much. However did you arrange this?"

"I've been doing a bit of research since our scavenger hunt. Turns out the New York State Festival of Balloons is held every September down in Dansville, so I made a few calls. I've booked us passage on a balloon called The Dream Weaver. Fitting, wouldn't you say?"

Polly's eyes burned with tears. "It sounds perfectly lovely."

He reached for her hand. "We're going to do this, Polly. And so many other things."

Oblivious to the carriage driver, who sang softly, waggling like a bobble-head, Sammy gave her a gentle kiss.

"I wish I knew how to thank you," she said. "I'm afraid my gift pales in comparison."

"Then give me another."

His speech dropped away into awkward silence and she gazed at him in curiosity. "And what would that be?"

"Something I asked you for many years ago." He faced her, his expression earnest. "Forgive an old fool for falling in love, Polly, but I'd like to marry you, if you'll have me."

When the words finally sank in, an overwhelming sense of joy filled every part of her. For in that moment, in the presence of this wonderful, caring man, surrounded by winking lights and tinkling sleigh bells, a future seemed not only possible, but wholly attainable.

She smiled. "I'll have you, Mister Delaney. I'd be honored to be your wife."

•

After Aunt Polly and Mr. Delaney left the gazebo, Wendy packed up the candy canes and the Hershey's kisses and turned off the lights. The darkly quiet night felt spooky after all the day's activity.

Over at the ice rink, Chase Alexander and a dark-haired woman were kissing, in a world all their own, and Wendy felt a pang of envy. Christmas time was the worst time of the whole entire year to be alone. Heck, even Aunt Polly had a lover.

The sound of music drifted to her on the evening air, pulling her footsteps toward the rec hall. Once there, she shouldered her way inside. The room was loud and crowded with people dancing and having fun.

She gazed toward the front and her breath caught. Brandon was absolutely stunning. Rocking and rolling, he looked like a god in his Santa hat and black tee shirt. His hands moved expertly over his guitar as he belted out *Santa Claus is coming to Town*, Bruce

Springsteen style. He was as sexy as they came. But standing there, watching him, she knew he wasn't for her. The only guy in the world she wanted wouldn't even talk to her. Her eyes moved to a far corner of the room, seeking Mick's. His eyes met hers for a heartbeat before he looked away.

The song ended with a flurry of guitar riffs and wild applause. Wendy was just considering heading over to the food tent for a sausage sandwich and a soda when Brandon's words stopped her in her tracks.

"I see my baby girl out there. My favorite little elf." Laughing, the crowd turned her way, and Wendy wanted to sink straight through the floorboards and disappear.

"A few weeks ago she gave me some songs to look at. She's a helluva song writer, and I say that sincerely. I was gonna save this one for later, but as long as she's here, why don't you folks give it up for my baby girl, Wendy!"

She stood there, disbelieving, as music once again filled the air. Her music. But it was different than she'd heard it in her head. She'd written the song in anger, but Brandon had put a different spin on it. The music had a desperate, haunting quality about it, as if he'd looked inside her heart and captured the essence of her sorrow.

I thought I was your baby
I thought I was your world.
I thought I was your everything.
I thought I was your girl.
Who would have thought
You'd turn my life into something
so crazy, something so cruel.
You broke this girl's heart
How could you be such a fool?

Her thoughts, her words, mingled with the wailing saxophone and the driving rhythm of Brandon's guitar. She felt naked. Ashamed. Why had she ever shared her songs with him? Why had she ever been born at all?

I was the one who loved you. I looked up to you, my hero.
Still you put me out in the cold, you made me feel like a zero.
Was it something I did? Was it something I lacked?
U lied, U hurt me, but still I'm wondering, baby, could we get it all back? I'm still wondering, baby, could we still get us back?

Mick's gaze met hers, anger and disbelief written all over his face. Eyes burning with tears of shame and humiliation, she turned and ran from the building. She raced down the pathway, feeling as if she wanted to run forever. She heard footsteps closing in behind her, and then they overtook her and Mick grabbed her arm.

"Where are you going?"

"Just leave me alone, Mick. I don't want to talk to you."

"Well I want to talk to you. I want to talk about that song."

"Why?"

"Who was it about? Me?"

"It doesn't matter now. I was wrong."

"About what?" he demanded.

"About what I thought I felt." She choked on the words, but forced them out. "I loved you, Mick. I really did. And you never even cared about me. If you did you wouldn't act the way you do. So let's just forget it, okay? Let's forget the whole stupid thing ever happened."

"Are you kidding?"

She lifted her hand and scrubbed the tears from her eyes.

"Are you kidding me right now?" His eyes blazed with an anger so fierce she had to look away from their scorching heat. "I act the way I act because I do care. I care a lot."

His words brought happiness and hope, but only for a moment. Aunt Polly had done her best to allay Wendy's worries, but still, the fear lingered like a dark shadow at the corners of her mind. "It doesn't matter now, anyway. I'm going to Philadelphia with Ms. Denning after Christmas. I may not be coming back."

"You're coming back."

"Aunt Polly's sick."

"What do you mean, sick?"

"She's got cancer. She's probably dying."

"If that happens, you'll come and live with us."

"I don't know what your dad would have to say about that."

"I don't care what he says. I'm not letting you go."

His words set her head spinning. For a moment she thought she'd faint.

"I thought you knew, Wendy. I thought you knew exactly how I feel. You're the one who ditched me. You started hanging out with all those low-life freaks, getting in trouble all the time. I tried to hang on, but I just felt you slipping farther and farther away from me."

"Don't even talk to me about that, Mick. We had it going on. I thought we had something special. And then you tell me you want to be friends." She laughed, a bitter, strangling sound.

"I do want to be friends, Wend. I want to be best friends. Because that's where it starts. And then it builds from there. And that way, nobody has to get hurt."

She looked at him then, took a good, long look, and saw a Mick she hadn't noticed before. A Mick who was as vulnerable and scared as she was. And she realized how selfish she'd been. She knew he struggled with depression, that he'd been hurt and betrayed, not just by a girl, but by his own mother. What she'd taken for indifference was merely his way of protecting himself. And she'd been too impatient, too selfish to wait for him.

"I'd like that, Mick," she said. "I really would."

He kissed her then—an earnest, awkward, sloppy kiss. It wasn't the romantic kiss she'd dreamed of when she first met him, the summer before. And it wasn't the fiery, passionate kiss she'd lied about in the girls' gym locker room. It wasn't the kiss she'd ached for so many nights, lying awake in her bed. Mick's kiss wasn't any of those kisses.

It was better.

Chapter Twenty-One

By the time Rachel breezed into the diner on Christmas Eve morning Lacy had already been there for an hour. She'd lit the oversized artificial tree in the dining room and set the radio to an oldies station that was playing nonstop Christmas music. She'd started the coffee urn and had just finished setting up the tables in her section for the morning crowd when Rachel walked through the door.

"Sorry I'm late." Rachel threw the apology over her shoulder as she strolled out back to change into her uniform. Ten minutes later she appeared in the dining room, pulling her hair back into an untidy ponytail. "I don't really think we should have to work at all today, if you want the truth. It's Christmas Eve, for heaven's sakes."

"Doreen's going to try and close up around one."

"I sure hope she does." Rachel grabbed up a stack of placemats and carried them to the tables in her section. "Some of us have better places to be today."

Lacy knew that was her cue to ask about Rachel's plans for the evening. She wasn't really interested, but she'd been trying to be nicer to Rachel lately. "I suppose you're doing something with Stan?"

Rachel shot her a coy grin. "I suppose."

"Okay, Rachel. What gives?"

"What do you mean?"

"You've obviously got a secret, and I'm too tired to try and guess. What's your news?"

"Oh, nothing much. Just this." She reached down the neck of her uniform and produced a shimmering cloisonné pendant on a thin gold chain. "Can you believe it?" she squealed.

Lacy studied the necklace. "What is it?"

"It's a cherry blossom," she said triumphantly, dropping the chain back into her blouse. "Do you have any idea what this means?"

Lacy pondered the possible meanings and came up blank. "Not really."

"It means that Stanley is going to propose to me. And probably tonight!"

Lacy stood there, still trying to connect the dots. "I don't get it."

Rachel sighed. "No, I wouldn't expect you to. You'd have to know about the mating rituals of the cedar waxwing, which I'm sure you don't."

Lacy grimaced. In the three short weeks that Rachel had been dating Stanley Maxwell, a conservation student at the university, she'd become an expert on birds, trees, wildlife, and just about every other area in the field.

"It's just romantic beyond belief," Rachel said, practically swooning. "Stanley told me that when the male waxwing wants to hook up with a female, he plucks a cherry blossom from a tree he's picked out for their nest and passes it to her. Then she passes it back, and they caress each other with their bills and whisper love songs and stuff. And Stanley gave me this cherry blossom necklace. What else could it possibly mean?"

Lacy's thoughts lingered for a moment on the caressing and the whispered love songs. She thought it very likely the gift meant that Stan was hoping to get lucky, but she didn't want to spoil Rachel's happiness by saying so. Instead, she said, "Well, it's a beautiful necklace, whatever it means. I'm happy for you, Rachel."

Throughout the morning, Rachel showed off her necklace to every customer she seated in her section. Lacy heard the story of the cedar waxwing's mating ritual so many times she thought she'd scream. But she knew the real reason for her irritation was jealousy. Rachel's persistence had finally paid off. At last she'd found her one and only love, a state of nirvana Lacy doubted she'd ever achieve.

She'd invited Chase over for a drink later that night, invited him over to say good-bye. The thought of it was more than she could bear.

After thinking about it long and hard, she'd decided to try and help God out. She'd gone to the ice skating rink and flirted

shamelessly, hoping to change Chase's mind about returning to
New York City. She didn't think she'd succeeded, but even so, the
evening had been pure magic. After the festival closed down for
the night, she'd invited Chase back to her apartment for a drink.
They'd spent hours watching the snow fall outside her window and
talking. About everything. About nothing at all. Chase Alexander
was the man she'd waited her entire life to find, and though she
hadn't known him for any for any length of time at all, she felt she
knew him profoundly. It was as if she was linked to him on a deep,
almost spiritual level. It was the first real connection she'd had
with another human being since Gretchen Kruger moved away.
She'd once thought she was in love with Angel, but that was merely
child's play compared to what she felt now. The last few days had
been the most wonderful and romantic of her life. She loved Chase
Alexander with her whole heart and soul. Which was why she had
to let him go. Tonight was about an ending, not a beginning, as
much as she might wish otherwise.

He's leaving in a few weeks, Lacy, she told herself. *And there's not
a thing you can do to change that, so there's no point in prolonging
the inevitable. It's time to move on, girl.*

By one o'clock the diner was empty except for one or two old
people who had nowhere better to be. Doreen called Lacy and
Rachel into her office and handed them each an envelope.

"What's this?" Rachel asked.

"Just a little something extra to show you girls how much I
appreciate you. Now get out of here." Rachel hit the door running
but Lacy stayed to help Doreen close up the diner. Unlike her co-
worker, she had no one to go home to.

At two o'clock, she walked slowly down the block, trying to
soak up some of the holiday cheer around her, taking note of the
twinkling lights, the tolling church bells, the shoppers who bustled
past, laden with last-minute purchases. Normally she loved the
undercurrent of excitement that only Christmas Eve could bring.
Today, she couldn't quite get there.

She shivered. She'd go home and put on her warmest sweater.
She'd brew up a batch of cider, using the mulling spices she'd bought
at the carnival. She'd light the Christmas tree Chase had bought for
her and insisted she put up. She'd go over the little goodbye speech
she'd prepared for him and when he arrived, she'd do her best to

put on a happy face and recite the lies.

With this decided, she trudged on toward home. She was halfway down Arbor Street, directly across from the Pawn Shop, when she noticed the large, red-and-white sign in the window of the abandoned bakery.

"What?" she whispered.

Heart pounding, she hurried toward it, certain her eyes must have deceived her. She stood on the sidewalk, blinking stupidly at the word, as if that would make it go away.

Sold!

"No," she said. "No!"

It wasn't possible. She'd walked past just this morning and everything had been the same as ever. It wasn't possible that her bakery was sold. She wouldn't let it be.

Her tears came slowly. They trickled down her face, leaving salty tracks before they froze to her eyelashes. In the air around her, the tolling of the church bells took on a mournful sound. They clashed and clanged, doleful, sorrowful, a requiem for her dying dream.

•

By time Chase arrived that evening, her eyes were red and puffed with tears. She'd shredded her book of affirmations, given up on her silly dreams. She'd stopped kidding herself and made herself face the facts. Fairy tales didn't come true after all. At least not for her. For now and forevermore, she'd be exactly what she was—a waitress and a part-time pastry chef. Not as brilliant a life as in her fantasies, but good enough for a poor girl from the wrong side of town.

Hearing a knock at her door, she splashed a handful of cool water on her face, straightened her clothes, and slid back the deadbolt. Chase stood in the entryway, snow glittering in his hair.

"Merry Christmas."

She forced a smile. "Back at ya."

She moved aside and ushered him in. "I made a batch of cider. Care for a mug?"

"Sounds good."

She moved to the kitchen, removed two mugs from the cupboard, and filled them, painfully aware of his presence only inches behind her. Squeezing her eyes closed, she took a breath.

Keep going, Lacy. You're doing fine.

Opening them again, she turned and handed him one of the mugs.

"I hope it's good. I've never made it before."

He took both mugs from her hands and set them on the counter.

"What's wrong, Lacy?"

"Nothing's wrong. Why would you think that?"

"Because I know you."

Her first thought was to deny it, to paste on a smile and carry out the pathetic charade. But why bother? She didn't have the strength, and in the end, the result would be the same, so she pulled in another breath and forced the words past her lips.

"The building is sold."

He studied her for a moment, realization dawning in his eyes. "The bakery?"

Clamping her lips into a tight line, she nodded.

"There are other buildings."

"Not like that one. Not with … Never mind. You don't understand."

"Yes, I do, Lacy. More than you think." He handed her a square, sloppily wrapped box.

"What's this?"

"Open it and see."

She tore off the paper and lifted the cover from the box. A pair of brass keys glinted at her from a small square of cotton. "Keys?"

"I bought the building."

Her eyes widened. "You what?"

"Working undercover narcotics is no kind of life. I'm thinking about going solo as a private eye. Maybe I'll start by trying to find out what happened to Moniqua Rodriguez. That office upstairs would be just about perfect. Unless you'd rather find an insurance agent."

She handed the keys back to him. "I can't accept these, Chase."

"Of course you can."

"I don't want to rent the bakery from you. I want to own it. I want … I need to do this on my own."

"The building is yours, Lacy; I'm just your bank. You can make monthly payments, whatever you're comfortable with."

"But it will take weeks to get the business up and running. Not to mention the weeks after that it will take to build a client base. I don't know how soon I'd even be able to make the smallest payments."

"Then you can pay me in doughnuts. I hear cops love 'em."

Beneath her tears, a deep, throaty laugh bubbled from her lips. Joy in its purest form washed over her and she felt as if she'd finally arrived at the place she'd spent her whole life searching for.

"Thank you, Chase. I know it's not enough to say, but it's the best I can do right now. You've made my dreams come true."

"I didn't make them come true, Lacy. I just helped them along a little bit."

"Why would you ..." Her voice caught. "Why would you do that for me?"

"I think you know the answer to that. Don't you?"

Tears burned her eyes. She didn't trust herself to answer.

"Growing up, I couldn't wait to get out of here. I thought of Sunset Cove as a small, shabby town with absolutely nothing to offer me. But in the past month I've realized there's nowhere else I really want to be. I've realized it's time to put down roots, maybe raise a family." His voice dropped. "And marry the girl of my dreams."

He cupped her face in his hands and kissed her again before gathering her into his embrace. Holding him close, Lacy knew that at last, beyond a shade of doubt, she'd found everything worth having in this world.

Chapter Twenty-Two

Maxine Perkins woke up at six o'clock on Christmas morning. After doing her daily stretches, she tiptoed down the stairs. When she reached the living room she couldn't resist lighting the tree, even though the hour was much too early. After she'd started a pot of coffee perking in the kitchen, she returned to the tree, sank down into her recliner, and pondered the stack of gifts beneath the tree.

Her gaze zeroed in on the large, oblong box in the center of the pile and she smiled, thinking of the warm, new jacket she'd bought for Chase. She made a mental tally of the other things she'd bought him; the insulated gloves, the hooded sweatshirt, the set of oversized coffee mugs and the blue sweater, the same lovely shade as his eyes. She hoped it was enough.

She heard the gurgle and whoosh of coffee perking in the next room and hoped the scent would wake him soon. She was as excited as if he were a little boy again, creeping down the stairs on Christmas morning.

Once she'd taken stock of his gifts, she eyed the packages he'd left there for her. Large packages in bold, bright papers. Obviously professionally wrapped. She hoped he hadn't gone overboard.

Her thoughts drifted to the housecoat he'd saved up his allowance to buy her as a ten-year-old. A God-awful, chartreuse-colored thing all made up of flannel and lace. How she and Willy had laughed, later that night, after Chase had gone to bed. Thoughts of Willy set her lip to quivering.

None of that, now, Maxine, she told herself.

After taking pause to acknowledge her sadness, she moved on to happier thoughts. Memories of Willy and the boys and the lifetime of love they'd shared in this house. Her eyes once again roamed over the gifts and her heart swelled. The best gift of all was not one that Chase could have wrapped up and placed beneath her tree. It was intangible, invaluable beyond her dreams.

He was staying.

She could hardly make herself believe it, but it was true. He'd bought an abandoned building on Arbor Street, a place with an office upstairs and a small apartment. He'd be moving in after the first of year. Maxine frowned. The place would need a good scrubbing from top to bottom. Her comments had all been positive on the day Chase took her through, but secretly, her hands had ached to scour and clean. Once she got at it she'd have the apartment ship-shape in no time.

Her brow creased again. He was welcome to stay on with her. Lord knew she had plenty of room. But she also knew a man needed his own space. Even so, she'd made him promise to come and have dinner with her at least twice a week.

Her thoughts drifted to the pretty, dark haired girl whose bakery would be occupying the lower level of building.

"She seems a nice sort," Maxine said out loud.

Maxine liked the sparkle in the girl's eyes, the warmth behind her smile when Chase had introduced them, and the way the girl had said, "It's very nice to meet you, Max."

Maxine thought she'd glimpsed a spark between the two young people, despite their formal greeting. But that was not for her to question. If there was news to be told, Chase would tell it to her in his own good time.

Hearing the creaking of floor boards upstairs, she smiled. He was stirring. Heaving herself from the chair, she went out to the kitchen to prepare his coffee. Dark and robust, just the way he liked it.

Snow fell outside her window, giving the street a lustrous, magical appearance and Maxine paused for a moment to soak it in. Her heart was filled with joy and a sense of optimism about the brand new year that was fast approaching. She couldn't imagine how it could be anything less than wonderful.

Her life hadn't gone according to the plan she'd made so many years before, but it had been a good life, a life worth living, just the same. She was sixty-four years old. An old woman by some standards, she supposed, but still young enough to make the most of the glorious adventure called life. She had a head full of memories and a heart filled with love. And she had Chase. Yes, like the gentle homing pigeon that travels miles and miles, but in the end returns, her lovely blue-eyed boy had finally come home to stay.

•••

See where it all started with M. Jean Pike's LOVE ON THE LAKE Series!

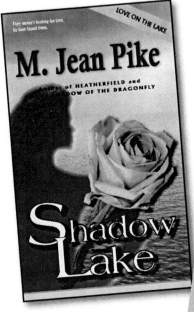

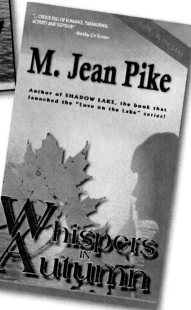

M. Jean Pike

Photo by Sharon Burr

Abandoned buildings. Restless spirits. Love that lasts forever. These are a few of M. Jean Pike's favorite things. A professional writer since 1996, Ms. Pike combines a passion for romance with a keen interest in the supernatural to bring readers unforgettable stories of life, love and the inner workings of the human heart. She writes from her home on a quiet country road in upstate New York.

www.freewebs.com/mjeanpike

CPSIA information can be obtained at www.ICGtesting.com
Printed in the USA
BVOW020132251111

276794BV00001B/11/P

9 781934 912416